Lucy

thank you for suppor___
being a fierce friend, and
being a light in this world.

The world needs more people
like you. And more terrible
joke Tuesdays.

xo

Waking Rory

Elizabeth Jeannel

HH
Hansen House

Copyright © Elizabeth Jeannel

Cover photography by Elizabeth Jeannel

ISBN 978-1-7353239-1-6 (paperback)

ISBN 978-1-7353239-0-9 (ebook)

First Edition

First Edition: July 2020

This paperback edition first published in 2020

Published by Hansen House

www.hansenhousebooks.com

Hansen House

Table of Contents

Acknowledgements

When I first started this story, I never could have imagined it would become what it is now, and it never would have without some incredibly key people in my life.

A lot changed for me when I joined a writing group on Discord. I made some amazing friends there, including Skye Kilean, JP Nadia, and Elka, who were so kind as to beta read this story in its first draft. They gave me advice and the moral boost I needed to make this a better story. Thank you. I couldn't have possibly finished this story without you.

I would also like to thank my editor, Kae Noble-Bray, who finished editing this story so quickly. You gave me the confidence to go forward.

Another thank you to my best friend, Lainie, who has forever been one of my biggest supporters.

Lastly, thank you to Kara, my wife, and the love of my life for putting up with everything that comes with each and every publishing journey.

*This book is dedicated to all those who dare to believe
in fairytales, magic, and happily ever after.*

"Mommy, read me a story!" I practically flipped into my bed, jumping on my knees on my lavender bedspread. I wasn't supposed to jump on the bed, but I was on my knees, so it didn't count.

My mom let out a sigh, but smiled as she carefully pulled the covers out from under me and tucked me in. It was late, well past my bed-time—as it usually was when I insisted on staying up until my dad came home from work. My mom let out a yawn, but turned and reached for a thick and worn book of fairytales she'd been reading from for months.

"Only one," she insisted, as she sat at the foot of my bed and waited for me to get comfortable before opening to where we'd left off the night before.

I pulled the covers up under my arms and wrapped my tiny fingers around a stuffed rabbit before clinging it to my chest. It was grey and faded and practically ripping at the seams. And it was still my favorite.

From the doorway, my dad stood watching with a slight grin tugging at the corners of his mouth. He looked tired too as he pulled his hands from deep in his pockets and crossed them casually over his chest, like he did when he was waiting for something.

"Once upon a time," my mom began, pulling my focus back to her, "A king and queen were blessed with a beautiful baby girl. Her name was Aurora, and she was beloved throughout all her kingdom."

My mom read through the story of Sleeping Beauty mostly as expected from what I'd already seen of the cartoon. There were tiny differences like no spinning wheel, and no prince dancing with her in the woods. But the ending really took me by surprise, as it often did with this particular book of fairytales.

"And then the princess, under the magical spell, fell into a deep sleep, where she would wait for a true love's kiss." My mom looked at me with a grin on her face. She loved reading these stories. "But the prince never came! And some say, Princess Aurora is still waiting."

"*Still?*" I nearly shrieked.

"That's what the story says." My mom shut the book and pulled the covers up to my chin. "Now, it's time for my little princess to fall under a sleeping spell herself."

I felt a yawn come on as my mom kissed my forehead and turned to put the book back on the shelf. The last thing I remember before drifting off was my dad's scruffy lip grazing my hairline before the light went out.

Chapter 1

The handcuffs hurt. I guess that was the point. They had to be so tight I couldn't slip out of them. Which wasn't putting anything past me, as I'd done that before. I'd been in more handcuffs than school desks that year, but it felt different this time. Something about this was more serious.

They were cutting into my skin to where I couldn't move, and every time I did, they only hurt more. I knew the guys were trying to get the message through, but I was getting a serious shoulder cramp, and it was almost 3AM, so I was actually ready for bed. Not to mention, I had the absolute worst itch on the tip of my nose just shy of my double nose ring.

It wasn't like I was some hardened criminal, anyway. All I'd done was a little underage drinking. In the park. On a school night. While putting my street art on a billboard. And, I know a crime is a crime, but the fact that I didn't stab or maim anyone like some of the jerks being dragged in there should have counted for something, right?

Whatever. It didn't matter anyway because my uncle, Nash, would be there any minute to bail me out like always.

But he wasn't.

I waited as minutes turned into an hour. And then two. And suddenly the tightness of the cuffs was making both my arms ache, but no matter how many times I asked to have them taken off, the officer behind the desk grinned like I was telling jokes. I kicked the floor with one of my Doc Martens, which only made him laugh. My butt was going numb.

The fuck was taking Nash so long? I knew they'd called him hours ago. I heard Jim, the juvenile officer, talking with him over the phone like they were pals. I guess he'd gotten acquainted with my uncle, too.

Of course, they had. Because Nash loved doing anything that made me unhappy. Like leaving me chained to a bench at the police station for three god damn hours.

I guess I deserved it. I never learned my lesson.

I sighed, "Hey, Matt." I called to the only officer whose name I knew. "Matty! My buddy! What does a girl got to do to get a glass of water around here?"

"Stay sober until she's 21." He grinned, and I heard a roar of laughter from the front desk. He continued to work through paperwork at his worn desk. I was pretty sure these guys had been there the first I'd been brought in.

I slumped forward, the layers of my brown hair slipping out of my low ponytail. Fuck these guys. 40-year-old virgins, I swear. Eh. Except Jim. His wife was nice. She took me shopping a couple of times, maybe trying to break the ice, warm up to me, be some type of mother figure. Christ, I didn't need a mother figure. I just needed my mom, and that wasn't possible. Still, I wasn't a little shit about it because I knew she was only trying to help.

I leaned back, wincing as my shoulders rested against the chipping white paint of the cinderblock wall. I could totally do it if I wanted. Stay sober, go to school, keep up my grades, be a perfect angel, but what was the point? I'd been there. I'd done that. I'd still lost everything that meant anything to me. And if nothing matters, which it fucking doesn't, then why try? Why bother? We all end up worm food in the end.

Besides, the only time I could stop reliving my nightmares over and over was when I was drunk or high. Usually, though, I had to be both. I knew I was playing a dangerous game, even being a minor with a rich uncle for a guardian. But it wasn't like I had much else to tame the demons in my head.

"You could get out of here sooner if you told us who you were with." I heard Jim's familiar voice echo down the hall. He should have gone home by now. Hell, I thought he had. What was he still doing here?

"*Captain* goes down with the ship, not the crew." I sighed, still trying to get comfortable.

"We both know you're not the captain of that crew, Even. I know they're your friends, but one of these days they're going to—"

"Get me into some serious trouble that Nash can't get me out of." I finished for him, looking up at the ceiling. "I know. I know. *They're always up to not good. I'm better than that.*"

"Why do you stick around them if you know they're always up to no good?" he said, coming closer as his steaming cup of coffee came into view. He was staying up—staying here—for me. His eyes looked tired. Shit, that made me feel guilty.

3

"I don't know." I shrugged. Would not be doing that again. Shrugging hurt. I winced, trying to sit up.

"I think you do."

Jim let out a tired sigh as he sat down on the bench next to me, set down his coffee, and pulled the cuff key out of his pocket. Matt rolled his eyes, trying not to look up at us from his paperwork, but I made sure to stick my tongue out at him anyway. At least someone cared about the ridiculous pain these cuffs were causing.

If they were going to go ahead and send me to juvi, sure I'd get it. But, if that were the case, they'd have done it by now, and Jim sure as hell wouldn't be sitting here waiting on Nash.

Once the cuffs were off, and I was rubbing my nearly numb hands together, Jim tilted his head toward the hall that held his office. "Why don't you come on back with me?"

I nodded and followed willingly, mostly because I felt guilty that he was here so late.

It didn't bother me with Matt or any of the other guys because they had to be here regardless. Graveyards were their shift. They were here every night whether I was arrested or not. It just so happened that nights were usually when I got into the most trouble. More importantly, they were when I got *caught.*

And it didn't usually bother me with Nash, either, because pretty much the only time he was home was on nights when I had gotten into some trouble. Forgive me for giving him a reason to use his bed. You'd think the pull-out couch at the office would hurt his back, but apparently, he's so loaded he can afford a comfy one.

But Jim? He had a wife and a four-year-old little girl who he didn't tuck into bed because of me. And, let me tell you, that ate at my usually ice-cold heart a little. At that age, my dad was everything to me, and if he didn't make it home before I went to bed, I couldn't sleep. Same for my mom, so I guess I felt guilty about his wife now, too.

Jim's office was small with a tiny desk, outdated computer, and a worn brown leather chair. If it didn't have floor-to-ceiling walls, it honestly could have been a cubicle, which seemed dangerous to me considering some of the juvenile delinquents were not so safe to sit down with in close quarters. But he clearly wasn't worried about that with me because he offered me a seat, and I took it.

"Even," Jim sighed, taking a careful sip of his still steaming cup of coffee, "I'm going to put it to you straight. I'm tired. Nash is tired. I really think you're on your last leg with this one. And you know you're only a year from eighteen."

I nodded.

"What I'm trying to say is that you really need to think about your future. What do you want to do with your life? Because there are some jobs that even juvenile records aren't sealed for. But, more importantly than that, if you get hooked with the wrong crowd, the wrong substances, in the wrong places, you could wind up dead, and that's not a case I look forward to seeing pass across my desk."

I swallowed hard. Jim had talked with me a lot over the last three years, given me talk after talk, but he never really told me I'd die. Shit, maybe I was on my last leg with him, too.

"I don't want to scare you, kid, but if that's what it takes that's what I have to do." He grunted, standing up, as I heard a shuffle at the door.

Nash.

I should have been excited—ecstatic. My hero had at last come to rescue me from this hell. But I wasn't. Nash wasn't a hero, and even when I *wasn't* in trouble, he never really seemed happy to see me. In fact, if I wasn't in trouble, I could go weeks without seeing his face, period. Maybe that's why I was always getting in trouble. It was the only time he was around.

I stood up and turned to face him. In the doorway to Jim's tiny office, my normally dashing uncle stood, no tie in his suit, his hair a little ruffled. He looked tired, and not in the way I was used to. His five o'clock shadow definitely looked like it was pushing 3AM. His brown eyes, the only real sign that we were related, didn't meet mine, but went straight to Jim, as he offered a less than firm handshake.

"Thanks, Jim." Nash said gruffly as Jim handed Nash my cell phone. I was clearly grounded from that. "Even, let's go."

He looked sad, and I pushed down the wave of guilt that came with the look he finally gave me. Jim reached my backpack and guitar case out to me, and I took them with a soft thank you, having to rushing catch up to Nash in the hallway.

As I slipped the strap of the guitar case over my shoulder, my shirt rode up nearly to my bra. Nash sighed, shaking his head, but he didn't say anything. He really was tired if he wasn't commenting on my clothes.

He was quiet, even as he led me out the front doors of the station, down the long path of steps, and to the waiting car, where Nash's driver was waiting.

"Gordon," Nash nodded as he stepped into the back seat.

Gordon held open the back door for us, and I waited, giving Gordon a quick hug that Nash didn't see.

"Thanks, G." I whispered.

Gordon nodded. He waited as I took the guitar and back pack off my shoulder and climbed in before he shut the door behind me.

As Gordon climbed into the driver's seat and put the car in drive, Nash cleared his throat, and I knew I was in for it. God, let me be back inside the police station. I'd take those handcuffs over what comes next any day.

Chapter 2

First of all, I hate cars, especially when it's dark outside. I'm almost always on foot; the only benefit I've found to Nash forcing me to live in the city. If I don't stare out the window during a car ride and count the parking meters, I'm likely to panic, or worst-case scenario, look at the oncoming headlights and black out. Which is why riding with Nash just means I piss him off.

Second of all, I hate being in cars when it's raining, snowing, or any other form of precipitation in which drivers might be poorly prepared for conditions. Which meant every day of the year for Seattle.

And third, I *really* hate being in cars with Nash, who is either yelling at me or talking on the phone. To be honest, I'm not always sure which he's doing most of the time because he rarely gives me an opportunity to respond anyway.

Nash was yelling this time, going on and on about how long of a day he'd had, how work was killing him, and how I'd cost him yet another relationship. *Good.* This girl was worse than the last. He'd been on the bad side of more publicity in the last month since they'd gotten together than he had been since he got custody of me. That was saying something, because I'd been on the front page after an arrest at least once.

That's what happens when your uncle/guardian is the head of a major international computer information systems company, and who makes friends with tons of celebrities. You're forced to attend social gatherings, red carpet events, philanthropist galas, and, oh yeah, you're constantly chased by the paparazzi. *And* you're expected to be an angel, paraded around like being at those events means your CEO head uncle is not only a great businessman, but also a great *dad.*

Of all the things Nash was, a good dad he was not. I'd had a good dad—no, I'd had the perfect dad.

Good dads didn't stay over at the office eight out of seven days a week. Good dads didn't send their *assistants* to parent-teacher conferences. Good dads didn't try to be a dad only when the cameras were flashing, disappearing for weeks on end when they weren't. Good dads didn't try to fix everything with money, ignoring that most of the problems couldn't be fixed.

Good dads didn't expect a child to make them proud while simultaneously not being around to *be* proud. Why try if no one's there to see it?

"Even, are you even listening to me?" Nash snapped, causing me to jump. Add to that, good dads didn't snap like that.

Gordon and I made eye contact through the rearview mirror, but he didn't say anything.

"Yeah." I nodded, though we both knew I wasn't. I was counting parking meters from the police station to the penthouse. It was usually how I tracked the time of these car rides.

"I'm serious this time." Nash continued, ignoring the fact that I hadn't been listening. "I had to work hard to get you this internship, so you had best not ruin it."

Internship? I looked over to Nash, who smiled a sly and damn near evil smile. He had my attention and he knew it. I hated when that worked. One big word like that, and I was all ears. Weakness maybe?

"There you are." He nodded sarcastically. If I did that, he'd probably smack me, but it's cool if he does.

I waited until he turned away to roll my eyes. Asshole.

Too many parking meters were passing by. We'd passed the penthouse. I had no idea where we were going. Maybe Gordon was driving in circles for all I knew. Truth be told, I barely knew Seattle despite running around wild for the last three years. I mostly followed my friends around, and I rarely went home the way I came.

"I know what you're doing, Even, and it's not going to work anymore."

I sighed.

"I will get through to you," Nash continued, but he knew he'd already lost my attention again.

I turned away from Nash to count the parking meters again, but there weren't any. We were heading out of town. I looked to Nash, who had finally gone quiet. Sure, now he didn't want to talk. Now that I was wide eyed and curious, he was all done.

Gordon pulled into Chance and Coy Airport a few moments later, and my stomach tied in knots.

Oh, shit. He was shipping me off to boarding school. Or military school. I couldn't decide which was a better option.

A few turns later, and we were under a rather large awning, with Autumn, Nash's assistant, beeming at me through the car window.

Autumn was rather underdressed that day, or as underdressed as Autumn ever was. Her hair was up in a messy bun, and she was wearing a t-shirt and dark wash jeans with her four-inch heels. Her makeup was done, but I could still see her freckles poking through on her nose, and the hairs falling out of her bun were a vibrant red.

She gave a swift wave. Why was she always in such a good mood? It was only 4AM. Who was in a good mood that early? Autumn, and the other Autumns of the world, that's who.

Gordon came around, and Autumn stepped back as Nash climbed out of the car. I didn't move. I didn't want to move. Maybe if I was quiet enough, I could hide in the trunk.

"Everything is set," Autumn said to Nash, as she checked something off the clipboard in her hands. "Anything else you need me to handle before we head out?"

"Just the luggage." Nash gestured to the suitcases and garment bag Gordon was grabbing from the trunk.

"And you already packed some things for Even?"

"We did what now?" I asked, looking between the two of them. They turned toward me like they might have forgotten I was there.

"You didn't tell her." Autumn sighed, reaching for the garment bag and suitcase Gordon had just set down next to Nash. "You handle that, and I'll have Gordon load these up on a cart for us."

11

Nash nodded, eyeing Autumn as she left. When his attention turned toward me, he cleared his throat and stuffed his hands in his pockets. He leaned his arm against the top of the door frame, looming over me. I hated how small that made me feel.

"I am headed to France for the summer to assist our branch there with their charity gala, and to work on a few other things." He let out a sigh. "And you're coming with me."

I opened my mouth to say something, but Nash held up his hand.

"You will be interning with the company for the next three months, and if you do well, we can discuss our plans for you in the fall. If you step out of line, you'll be attending boarding school in the fall."

I swallowed hard.

"And, if you get into any trouble while in France," He sighed. "You'll be headed right back here, spending the rest of the summer in juvi. Sound good?"

I looked down.

"Answer." He snapped. It wasn't angry, really. He was just tired. I think in his own way, he was trying to teach me something about respect, but he was going about it wrong.

"Okay." I muttered.

He scoffed. "'Okay.'"

"What?" I asked. "That not a good enough answer for you?"

His jaw tensed, but he dropped his voice down almost to a whisper. Too many business types around, maybe. "You think I get away with 'okay' to my colleagues?"

I shrugged. I wasn't his colleague. I noticed his knuckles were whitening with the grip he had on the door. I really needed to quit the Nash button-pushing game.

"So we are clear, 'okay' is not an acceptable answer."

I let out a sigh. I didn't even mean to, it just slipped out.

"You're pushing it, Even." he growled. "You need to wise up. The way you act is disgraceful, not only to me, but to your parents and their memory. Do you know how absolutely disappointed they'd be knowing all the trouble you've been in, drinking, doing drugs—"

"It was just weed. It was one time."

"I know about the pills, Even. I'm not stupid."

I looked down at my chipped, black nail polish and clenched my teeth. *The pills.* Depression medication that I bought from someone at school. My one attempt at a healthier form of self-care, and he was pretending he didn't know I wasn't popping pain killers or Xanax.

"Your parents didn't raise a criminal or a druggie. Is that what you want? To be a homeless addict, living on the streets, selling themselves for a hit? Because hanging out with the people you do, that's where you're headed."

"I'm not a druggie."

"What do you call someone who does illegal substances?"

It was like talking to a brick wall. I shrugged. He fumed.

"Disappointed doesn't even begin to cover it at this point." He sighed, apparently letting the anger dissipate. "I'm surprised at you, drinking. With what happened to your parents, I'm surprised you touch the stuff."

He had a lot of room to talk. He had whiskey everywhere, including the car. I eyed it, he followed my gaze and let out a sigh. When I looked back up at him his face had softened slightly. He reached into his pocket and pulled out a small device, tossing it my way.

I examined it. "This is a kid's phone."

"Yeah, you're right." He nodded, grinning wide. "I'm going to treat you like a child until you start acting your age. It only makes calls to me, your boss, and emergency numbers. Let's go."

Chapter 3

If you've never been to a private airport, there's a few things you should know. It's not super fancy, lavish, or overly decorated, and most of the benefits of using them are for pilots. The only real benefit is the lack of line, lack of baggage checking, lack of, well much of any major security. From the moment Gordon pulled into Coy and Chance Airstrip, to the moment I was buckling in across from Nash, it couldn't have been more than fifteen minutes.

There wasn't a lot of waiting in line, no TSA searches, and I'm pretty sure they didn't even check our bags. Which was good because I'd put my cigarettes in my guitar case, and my fake ID was tucked into my bra.

Nash handed some paperwork to the desk clerk, and we were sent to our terminal. The McCoy terminal, only used by the McCoy plane. I couldn't even imagine how much it cost to keep his name on *that* parking space. If I was honest, I didn't want to know.

As we made our way across toward the white and maroon vessel, our tiny crew seemed already to take off. A single attendant took my bags, but I insisted the guitar and backpack stay with me. Nash didn't notice. Our pilot was speaking with some of the staff from the airstrip outside. Nash and Autumn headed right toward the stairs and onto the plane.

I looked up at it for a moment. The *Miranda*. Conveniently named after my mother, but I'm pretty sure this wasn't the original McCoy plane. My dad, a rather skilled pilot, had loved to take my mom out *for fun*. But his plane had been smaller than this, or so I thought. I'd only ever seen photos.

"Even?" I heard Nash call from inside, a slight hint of worry in his voice, though I couldn't be sure. I don't think he'd ever been worried about me.

"Coming," I called.

I climbed into the plane behind them, holding tightly to my backpack and guitar. Inside, the seats were maroon to match the exterior lettering, as was the carpet floor, and the exterior of the compartments.

With a large amount of effort, I choked down a scoff at Nash, who already had a glass in his hand full of dark brown liquid. Whiskey? Brandy? Couldn't be sure, but I didn't really care. He was always drinking, which only made his anger at *my* drinking seem misplaced.

"What?" he asked, as if I'd said the words aloud.

"Nothing." I shrugged. "Where do I sit?"

The plane had a total of twelve seats, all placed well apart with the ability to turn and face the group for better conversation. I only hoped Nash didn't expect me to *speak* to him on this flight. Twelve hours. I had twelve hours in a

16

confined space with my uncle, with whom I'd long ago run out of things to talk about. Safe topics anyway.

"Wherever you'd like." He gestured. "It's just us."

Perfect.

Autumn sat toward the back, her computer already out, along with some files she was working on. I chose a spot in the middle, knowing he'd likely choose one close to me. Of course, I was right. Once I'd made myself comfortable and the pilot stepped onto the plane, Nash took a seat directly across from me.

Something about the way he was sitting, his jacket unbuttoned, his tie nowhere in sight, and his posture less rigid, gave me hope that maybe, just maybe, this flight wouldn't be so bad. He opened his mouth as if to say something, but sighed and closed it again, leaning back in his chair.

"You'd best buckle in," he said, pulling out his computer. Typical.

The pilot gave the usual spiel, and within a few minutes we were prepping to take off.

Planes were the worst. As we began lining up with the runway, I started my grounding ritual, but I had to do it a total of twelve times before we were in the air. What could I see? What could I smell? What could I hear? What could I taste? What could I feel?

The last thing I needed was to have a panic attack on a plane with *Nash*.

Take-off was smooth, despite all the fear I had about it. It was quick, but it still made my ears pop and gave me a pressure headache. Nash didn't seem bothered at all; he kept typing on his computer like nothing had even happened. I guess when you fly twice a week you get used to it. I didn't feel like I'd ever be used to it.

The silence on the plane was deafening. The only sound was that of Nash and Autumn typing away on their computers. I didn't know either of them well enough to know if it was safe to watch a movie while they worked. So, I pulled out a book instead.

This grabbed Nash's attention. He looked over with a raised eyebrow as I pulled the book from my backpack. As if someone who causes trouble on a daily basis can't make time to *read.* Joke was on him, I read stories that taught me how to cause trouble.

I didn't feel safe getting out my sketchbook here. It was mostly sad sketches and poetry, but that didn't mean I wanted him reading any of it.

At some point, I dozed off. It had been a long night, after all, and we were headed to an entirely different time zone. I wasn't prepared for Nash or Autumn to see just why I stayed out at night—why I got so little sleep and needed to drink to numb the pain.

The thing about trauma is that no matter how far you are from it, no matter how much you try to move on, it's still buried deep in your subconscious. You know where you go when you dream? Your subconscious. And, as it turns out, mine liked to take me back to the worst night of my entire life, over and over.

I was in the car—my parents' car. I could feel the metal crushing in around me. Through the tiny hole near the window, I could scarcely see anything. All around me was silence.

In the distance, I caught a glimpse of something— something moving. It had an orange glow about it. It was something near the size of a coconut, and it was buzzing through the air. It zipped about, like a bug might do.

I blinked a few times. The orb was getting closer to the car now. There was something faintly familiar about it.

As it grew closer, the tightness of the metal around me seemed to intensify. It felt like a giant had taken ahold of the car and was squeezing it tight. I couldn't move my arms anymore. I could barely breathe.

I was going to die.

<hr />

I writhed against the grip on my arm shaking me awake as I looked up at Nash standing over me. My face was wet. Hell, my whole body was wet. I was breathing really fast. I looked around.

I could see the maroon seats, feel the blanket around me, smell Nash's cologne, taste the sweat from my upper lip, and hear the roar of the wind outside the plane windows. My breath slowed. I swallowed hard.

"Even, it's only a dream, you okay?" Nash's face was twisted with concern. He almost looked like he was going to hug me. Nash didn't hug.

"I'm fine." I shrugged, standing up, forcing him to step back. "Where's the bathroom?"

"Toward the back," he said numbly, "Even, if you need to t—"

"I'm fine." I snapped, rushing toward the back of the plane, passing Autumn, who looked up with wide eyes but didn't say anything.

I would not let them see me cry.

"Even," Nash called after me, softly, a tone of voice that didn't even sound like him. "That wasn't fine, but I think you know that."

I did, but I wasn't going to admit that to him.

"Can you please talk to me?"

I stopped, just shy of the bathroom door, and turned. I knew there were tears in my eyes, and I wasn't sure if I cared anymore. He'd already seen me crying anyway. "I guess now you get why I do the drinking, huh?"

I stepped into the bathroom and slammed the door shut behind me.

Chapter 4

"Even, you can't stay in there the rest of the flight. We still have four hours left." Nash's muffled voice echoed through the cracks in the door of the small plane bathroom.

For a while, Nash had given me some space, but he was back. From the sound of his voice, he was standing across the small hallway. I'd been sobbing for the better part of an hour. Partly out of embarrassment and partly from the emotions that always came when I had that dream.

I knew both Nash and Autumn could hear me. It's not like we were in a huge plane, and the walls were paper thin. The only saving grace was the endless sound of the wind outside, but even that wasn't as loud as I'd remembered it as a kid. I had just reached a very specific form of mental exhaustion where the embarrassed side of me lost to the side of me that needed to fall apart.

"Don't you have something better to do?" I replied, wiping the mascara that had been rubbed all the way up to my left eyebrow ring. "Go take a phone call or answer an email."

I heard an exaggerated sigh. "The calls can wait."

That was a first. I opened the door to the bathroom before I thought better of it. "Why?"

Nash was standing in front of me, jacket removed, leaning against the wall across from the bathroom, looking more casual than I'd seen him in years. He didn't look angry, but more importantly, he didn't look drunk. It was, most likely, the first time Nash had ever looked concerned.

"Because…" He paused, letting out the nervous hitch in his breath. "I feel like we need to talk."

"About the nightmares?" I asked. "Because I've had them for years. It's always the same, and there's nothing you can do about it."

"You should have told me."

"When? You weren't ever home."

He stiffened. That hurt, clearly.

"If I'd known you were dealing with trauma after the accident, I would have—"

"What, Nash?" I scoffed. "You would have tucked me in every night, made me breakfast each morning, been a dad?"

"Even—"

"No, you know, what? I get it. I'm a burden on you, and you can't wait to be rid of me."

"No, that's not—"

"Do you even know what happened in the accident?" I was eyeing him, for a hint of recognition.

He shook his head.

"I was pinned in the backseat floorboard for over six hours before anyone drove down that road." He looked up, eyeing me intently. "Mom died instantly, but Dad could've—they said he was—and I could hear him. He couldn't move, but he was looking for me, Nash. And I couldn't—"

Nash reached to me, and I let him. I let him wrap me up in a hug that made me feel at home again. He was so much like my dad in so many ways despite how much he wasn't. And I just sobbed like that, Nash holding onto me for dear life.

When we landed in Lyon, France, it was 1AM. Which was perfect for me, because I was exhausted. Gordon had stayed behind in Seattle, which meant we had a temporary driver in France. I hated new drivers. I could barely stand it when Gordon took a day off, much less dealing with someone entirely new for the summer.

He wasn't a bad driver, though. And he was quiet, didn't take his eyes off the road.

He dropped Autumn off at a hotel, but Nash wouldn't let me out of the car. Instead, he insisted I stay, and the driver took us toward the house we'd be staying in.

It was raining, coming down in fits. Nash talked briefly in the car about getting a quick nap in before we had to be up for work. With how wet it was, I could have been fooled into believing we'd never left Seattle at all. Except for the architecture, which was much too beautiful even in the dark to have possibly been in Seattle.

He seemed different after the plane. Not once from the moment I woke up from that nightmare to the time I was climbing into the car with him did Nash take a phone call. He was watching me. For once, he was the concerned uncle he should have been all along, and I hated it. I'd grown accustomed to loneliness.

Inside the house was beautiful in that modern way. Everything was white or black, tall ceilings, sleek lines. It was like Nash had brought his apartment with him. There was a small kitchen, three bedrooms, and two bathrooms, much more than the average vacationer could hope for. The living room was filled with practically brand-new furniture, and at the center, a large piano. I rolled my eyes.

Nash loved putting me around pianos. He'd even taken the liberty of buying one for his own apartment, so that I might use it if I wanted. If I had my way, I'd never touch the piano again.

I scoffed and heaved my bag and guitar past the piano toward the hall. I left the biggest room for Nash. It had it's own bathroom and a massive king sized bed. I settled for the smaller one up the hall, closer to the front door, with a whole bedroom between me and him to grant me at least one ounce of privacy.

Nash didn't say anything else as he headed down the hall to the larger room. I crashed on the bed without even unpacking.

Chapter 5

I was deep in the woods again, sitting on top of a large log, looking out at the sunrays slipping between leaves. A set of hands covered my eyes. It was playful like kids do, and I felt a grin spread across my lips as she whispered "Guess who?" in a voice so familiar.

A flash of golden hair and porcelain skin danced around toward me, as her fingertips trailed the length of my arm to my hand. She was pulling me onto my feet, and we started...spinning?

No, dancing. I was dancing. I'd never been much of a dancer. High school dances weren't cool to hipster kids who thought the only thrills in life came from a light or a bottle. But this was nice. It was...soothing turning around and around.

I'd been here before, or so I thought. This place, these woods, these arms; they were so familiar to me. They felt like home, or what I thought home might feel like these days. I'd forgotten, it had been so long.

I looked down; two bright eyes looked back. They were so familiar, and my eyes trailed to a smile that made my stomach tie in knots.

"Even," I heard a voice say, softly, soothingly. "Come find me."

And then she was out of my arms, dancing off into the woods by herself.

I opened my eyes to a nearly pitch-black room. The dream lingered in my mind as the feeling of home slowly faded. I'd had the dream before, but I was dreaming about her more now. And every time I woke from one of those dreams, I found myself with this ridiculous sense of hope that she was out there somewhere, just waiting for me.

A sigh escaped my lips as I rolled over, hoping maybe I could get back to sleep. But when I closed my eyes, the only thing I could see were hers.

"Even," Nash called, poking his head in my room. "Get up and get changed. Hurry or we'll be late, and don't forget to take out those awful piercings."

I groaned, rolling over in the bed. The sun still wasn't completely up, why did we need to be? Nash closed the door and slipped out, expecting me to be dashing about like he was, but my head was still stuck in the woods with those eyes.

I'd had dreams like that before. They weren't always the same, but she was. The same golden hair, the same blue eyes, the same smile. I had to know her from somewhere. I had to.

Nash knocked on my door again for good measure as he headed back to his room from the kitchen. I groaned again. Not only was I not looking forward to the internship period, I was also tired. That wasn't exactly the longest nap, and I'd not gotten much sleep on the plane, which meant not only was I jet lagged, I was just tired in general. Nash, however, was all hype. What kind of coffee did he drink? And why wasn't he sharing?

I rolled out of bed and dug through the suitcase Nash had packed. Who let this man think that was okay? Not a single regular bra, only sports bras, and he packed twelve of them. Rather than bothering packing underwear, it looked like he'd had Autumn stop and buy me knew ones by the tags and the fact that I'd never seen them before.

I don't think he'd even paid attention to what he'd grabbed. A few pairs of jeans I'd never worn before, some basic t-shirts I'd meant to donate because they were too small, and a single jacket. I let out a sigh and slipped on the first thing I found, spitefully grateful that it was wrinkly. The shirt was far too tight and short, but he'd packed it.

Then, equally out of spite, I changed my double nose and eyebrow ring to clear plastic ones. No way was I leaving them empty all day. It wasn't like people wouldn't notice the gaping holes in my face.

When I stepped into the hall, Nash paled.

"Good lord, do you not own a single shirt that covers your midsection?" He scoffed, pulling his own jacket off and shoving it in my direction.

"You packed them." I let out a laugh, pushing his jacket back to him. "I probably could have packed something more *presentable* myself."

"Well, I didn't really have time for that, now did I?"

He followed me down the hallway as he struggled with whether he was going to put his suit jacket back on or try and force me to wear it. He must have decided on the former, because it didn't slip over my shoulders when I stepped into the kitchen and grabbed an apple from the fruit basket on the table.

"Maybe we could have used the three hours I sat in the police station." I grinned as I took a bite from the apple.

He glared at me as he slipped his jacket back over his shoulders, but there was a smirk playing at the corners of his mouth. He was terrible at this parenting thing. So terrible, in fact, that he couldn't even be mad that I'd been arrested for more than a day. His brain was always so occupied with other things. Out of sight, out of mind. Maybe that's why he brought me this summer. Seeing me all the time just might keep me on his mind.

"I was busy," he said quickly, putting together some papers on the table and slipping them into his briefcase. God, he hadn't even slept.

"Busy, huh?" I asked with my mouthful of another bite. "You enjoyed leaving me cuffed to that bench, admit it."

"I'll admit," he sighed, "that I thought the longevity of the wait would be a good reminder of what your life could look like if you didn't do well this summer."

I nodded, munching on the apple to the core.

"Let's get going. Autumn is going to have to find you something else to wear."

That was the closest to a genuine conversation we'd had in months. Usually it was one sided. Him yelling, me pretending to listen, which made him yell more. We never *talked*. Not like this. Shit, things were weird since the plane.

I let out a sigh and headed to my room for my backpack before following him out to the car. I was never far from my sketchbook, and some internship in France wasn't about to change that.

The urge to grab my guitar hit me as I turned toward the door, but I knew better. Nash would have a hayday with that one.

⌘

Autumn was ecstatic about shopping. She lived for heading out on a big spree, and shopping in France? That was her literal dream, even if she wasn't shopping for herself. Or maybe spending someone else's money was part of the hype. I wasn't sure.

The only shopping that got me off like that was shopping for art supplies.

I, personally, could be more than happy only buying things online for the rest of my life. Large crowds, packed lines, and fitting rooms are all on the list of things I'd rather avoid.

Nash had the driver drop the three of us of at a large shopping center. After which Nash headed off to make a phone call, while Autumn and I did the actual shopping.

It was still pretty dark outside, and there was no one else here apart from the single person who held the door for us. Which made me wonder if Nash had called in some sort of favor. What time did these places open, anyway?

"Even, come on!" Autumn called, and I had to jog to catch up with her.

She led me to racks and racks of button-downs, jackets, dress pants, and so many blouses it made me dizzy. None of it was my style, but I guess that was the point. My style didn't exactly belong in a business setting.

Autumn began loading up my arms with sweaters, blouses, and skirts. She grabbed a couple dresses and sent me off to the changing room.

A couple times she made me change shirts. Something about the blouse being the wrong fabric with the pants. It made no sense to me, but after I'd tried on a handful of things, she seemed mostly content.

She grabbed the things she thought went well, and led me to a rack of jackets.

I looked around at the clothes around me. So many rules about clothing. Who decided all this, anyway? Were there actual fashion police? Or were people just making these rules up as they went along?

I let out a sigh. This was so overwhelming.

"You know he's only doing this because he wants what's best for you, right?" Autumn asked.

"I'm sure he is." I sighed again.

"He really loves you; you know."

"Does he?"

She frowned. "Of course, why—"

"Well, he doesn't ever say it, so." I breathed. "Can we just—can we just finish shopping and go? No offence, Autumn, I mean…shopping's not really my thing."

"Not when it's anything but rocker tees, huh?"

I let out a playful scoff. Why Autumn put up with my uncle, I'd never know.

I slid my feet into the awful heels that Autumn had insisted would be my every-day wear and eyed myself in the mirror. I looked like a McCoy. Gross.

For years, I'd insisted I was *just Even*. None of that 'Miss McCoy' nonsense. If growing up did anything for me, I hoped it allowed me to simply be me. Because even to my friends back home, I wasn't just Even. I was still Even McCoy, yes that McCoy.

I'd have given anything to drop the last name and be somebody else. Maybe that's why I was single. Any time I told a girl my name, that was the end of it. And it's not like the name Even really did me any favors, anyway.

"Even, we really have to get going!" Nash called through the changing room door.

"I'm almost done!" I called back, tossing my chest length hair up into a ponytail.

It was ratty and gross, but that's what happens when you rush. I looked like a mess. A full-on mess. My makeup wasn't done, and he hadn't packed any remover, so water had done a less than adequate job of removing what was left from yesterday. I looked less like his niece and more like some homeless girl he'd picked up on the street and shoved into nice clothes. I didn't know if I even cared.

I cared.

And yet, I just marched out of the fitting room and met him in the doorway. He gave me a puzzled expression, probably at my lack of raccoon eyes, as he called them. I shrugged and followed him and Autumn wordlessly through the pouring rain toward the car.

⨒

We pulled up in front of a familiar building. The Lyon branch of McCoy Enterprises was identical to the one in Seattle, including all the rain. I'd heard it was also identical to the one in Chicago and New York, but I couldn't be sure. This one was shorter, though. It couldn't have been more than 30 stories.

It was a charcoal grey with hundreds of windows and big, bold, brass letters that read "McCoy Enterprises."

Nash got out, and I followed, still not used to everything being on the opposite side of the road. Outside the car, there was a bustle of business people coming and going, sheltered from the storm only by umbrellas just like in Seattle. But unlike in Seattle, I understood a total of five words per person. Shit, I wished I'd paid more attention in French class. They were all speaking so quickly.

I wouldn't last one day in this place.

"Even, come on, we'll be late," Nash called.

I followed him inside, tugging at the sleeve to my baby blue button-down. It wasn't long enough. You could see my scars on my wrist. I hated it almost as much as the blazer I'd put over it, but at least the blazer and pants were black. If only I hadn't been given heels as everyday wear.

I'd be buying flats the first chance I got. My toes already hurt, and you could see the scars on my feet in them too.

Inside was the same sort of bustle I was used to walking into the business in Seattle. The entry was laid out the same, with security in the same posts and elevators in the same place.

The only real difference was the lack of English. I was toast. Burnt toast.

"*Monsieur* McCoy," A tall blonde woman called to us, and Nash went to her with a smile.

They began speaking like old friends, murmuring to one another like they didn't know I had no clue what they were saying. There was a laugh, then they were looking to me.

"What?" I asked, looking from Nash to the woman.

"Didn't you—" Nash took a deep breath, walking over to me, and calling, "*Pardòn*" over his shoulder. "Were you not listening to what we said at all?"

I breathed, eyeing him like he was an absolute lunatic. "Listening? I heard Mister, good morning, and work."

"You don't..." He let out a deep sigh. "Didn't you just take French?"

"One year of *high school* French, Nash." I breathed, eyeing the people around us whose attention had fallen on us. "And I barely passed."

He groaned. A hitch in his magical summer plans, I was guessing. But it didn't make me happy like it should have, because having to spend a summer working with people I couldn't understand and couldn't understand me was most definitely the worst punishment he ever could have dished out.

I rode with Nash to the top floor. It was awful, but not nearly as bad as the headquarters in Seattle. I still wasn't brave enough to think I could take the stairs everyday, but the idea of the leg muscle I'd have at the end of the summer was appealing.

Nash led me past the lobby, where the receptionist ogled at him on his way through. We walked past several sets of meeting rooms, and cubical set-up, until Nash stopped at the entry to an open office. Once there, I realized not speaking French was the least of my problems.

I knew immediately walking into the room who was in charge. A tall, slender woman, who's business suit was pressed, her lips pursed, and her voice shrill. She had an unusually tight bun on the top of her head, and it only made her long neck seem longer. When her eyes fell on me, I was pretty sure she was cutting through me with them. I had ruined her morning just by showing up.

"Even, this is Madam Caron," Nash smiled. "She will be in charge of your internship."

"*Ravi de vous rencontrer, Mademoiselle McCoy.*" She said with a rather exaggerated flare.

Shit. *Shit.* Say something. Anything. Oh God, she was intimidating. I wasn't even completely sure what she'd said. Nice to meet me, I thought. Oh eff, what was I supposed to say?

Nash stepped in, breaking the woman's eye contact with me. He began rattling off in French. I could only pick up every few words. He was saying something about school, I knew that. Something was little…oh, my French-speaking ability was little.

She looked back to me, and her eyes narrowed. I was dead meat. Why, Nash? Why were you doing this to me? I knew I was a little ungrateful shit sometimes, but this was a fate worse than death.

"I see, should not be a problem," the woman spoke. Clearly speaking English wasn't an issue, and she was testing me. I failed. Back to Seattle for me. Jail it is, please. "We will find her, eh...something."

That sounded awful to me, but Nash seemed pleased. He turned, gave me a squeeze on the shoulder, and headed toward the other side of the floor, leaving me standing in front of this tall, intimidating woman.

I eyed him for only a moment as he shook hands with another well-dressed man and ducked into a conference room.

"*Follow me, mon chéri.*" Madame Caron said quickly, sarcastically.

I did without a word.

She led me past a number of desks where people were answering phones. *Oh, please don't let me have a phone.* Toward the back, the furthest from the door, the windows, and the bathroom, was the tiniest desk I'd seen in a workplace. On it was a large stack of documents.

"You are lucky our last American intern had to quit," she said flatly. "These documents are in English. You are to check they are...how you say, grammatical correct."

That wasn't how we said, but I definitely wouldn't correct her on it. I nodded.

"I trust your English is better than your French, no?" She raised an eyebrow at me, which only made her *more* intimidating.

"No," I nodded. "I mean, yes. My English is better than my French."

"*Parfaite.*" She smiled, and oh, did she enjoy this. "I will leave you to it."

I took my seat, but she didn't move.

"Let me be clear, *mademoiselle*," she said softly, but it was still cutting through me like a knife, "I am not happy to have you here. There are many who deserve to be here much more than you. And I will happily send you on your way should the opportunity present itself."

I swallowed, nodding. "I wouldn't expect any less, Madame."

Her lip twitched slightly, like she might have smiled. Instead she turned, heading back toward where Nash had found her.

I let out a sigh, scanning the desk around me. It had a computer. Nash was smart with the whole phone thing, trying to keep me from having contact with my friends, but I guess he didn't consider I'd be an intern with a desk, and a computer that had Internet access.

And like any obnoxious kid my age, the first thing I did when I had the chance was go back to old habits.

The computer wasn't locked. It didn't take a special passcode. Social media wasn't locked out, and I didn't need a WIFI password to get online. It took me less than two minutes to pull up my page and send a message to my best friend Molly.

Hiding the fact that I was doing it while pretending to edit these stupid documents with my boss pacing back and forth was a little more difficult. I waited nearly thirty minutes with the page pulled up for her to read my message and respond. She didn't.

My lunch break was worse than high school. There was a break room somewhere in this building, I was sure of it, but I wasn't brave enough to go find it. Especially when I noticed that a large portion of the people in the office had ordered in.

I didn't have any money, so I couldn't do that. Instead, I stayed at my desk and pretended to keep working.

The words on the page had started to bleed together a while ago, and I was pretty sure there was nothing wrong with half these documents anyway. I'd only found a total of six errors in all fifteen documents I'd looked over so far. I was only hoping that I wasn't wrong. Heaven help me if Madame Caron found out I couldn't even read English right.

I was just about to go cry in the bathroom when Nash walked out of the conference room. The entire room seemed to hush. Everyone knew him, which was both good and bad for me. That meant that everyone expected a lot from me, and I was pretty much useless.

Nash walked straight toward me, an unusual expression on his face. "Even, what are you doing?"

"My job?" I shrugged, holding up one of the documents that I'd begun reading.

"You were supposed to meet me at the elevators fifteen minutes ago. Let's get some lunch."

"No one told me that."

"Maybe you should check your phone." He laughed lightly. This was funny to him, this phone thing.

"I think I left it at the house," I said, wincing as I stood. These heels were the absolute worst.

"We can grab it on our way through. Come on."

I followed him back out of the office, feeling the eyes of several of the girls there. Oh, my God, they were checking him out. And giving me the stink eye. Gross, I'm his niece, but I had a feeling some of them didn't know that. Or maybe they didn't care.

Word had probably already gotten out that he was single again. Not that most women who knew who Nash was cared much about that. But when he was single, women were clingy, overly nice, incredibly flirty. And Nash? Nash was oblivious.

"How's your day so far?" Nash asked as we climbed into the elevator.

I forced myself not to shrug or roll my eyes. "She's giving me busy work, so I guess it could be worse."

"Everyone's job here is important, Even."

I nodded. "Of course."

"Have you learned anything new yet?" he said, as the doors opened and we stepped into the busy entryway.

"Yeah, I really suck at business jargon." I sighed. God, I hated big crowds.

Nash laughed. He actually laughed. At least someone was enjoying their day.

"You'll get better at it," he insisted as we reached the car. "I'm sure you'll be using it like me in no time."

I didn't like the way he said that. Something about his tone, maybe. Something about it lingered between us. Like there was some hidden meaning behind it.

I was still debating whether this was worse than jail in Seattle when I got back from lunch. Something about McCoy Enterprises felt like a prison to me. Still, I made my way back through the lobby, to the elevator, and pushed number 33. At least the numbers were the same in French.

Once in the office, I quickly went back to my seat. Partly because I didn't want to be yelled at by my scary boss, but also because I wasn't a fan of the looks I was still getting from the other girls there.

He's my uncle. I thought to myself, but I didn't think that would matter. Uncle or not, I'd only gotten this job because of him, and that was probably enough to make most of them hate me. Hell, it kind of made me hate me.

As my desk came into view, my boss was standing over it, looking over the work I'd done so far. Thank God I'd closed out the computer. I couldn't imagine what she would have done had she seen that.

"Ah," she breathed, barely looking up. "How was your first French meal?"

"Good." I nodded, feeling my throat get tight.

"Your work ethic, not so much, eh?"

I wasn't sure what that meant, but I figured it probably wasn't good.

"Read these again, I think you missed something." She slammed the documents down on my desk, causing me to jump and sauntered past me. She looked fierce walking in heels. I looked like a new born goat. I looked up at the ceiling, letting out a sigh.

I wasn't cut out for this.

I spent the rest of the afternoon rereading the documents I'd already done, and still couldn't find anything else wrong with them. I was on the verge of tears by the time my phone buzzed in my pocket. I knew there were only two people who could have possibly sent me a message, so I braced myself for whatever came my way.

"Should be down to get you in fifteen. Almost ready to go?" Having Nash around more should have made me happy, but it just seemed odd.

"Yeah." I sent back, but I wasn't really sure about that.

No one else seemed to be ready to end their day. Phones were still ringing, and papers were still being printed. My boss was still stalking around the room being rather theatrical about the orders she barked to every assistant, intern, and employee in the room. When she finally made her way to me, I felt myself stiffen.

"Do you have any documents for me?" she asked, holding out her hand.

I presented her with the documents, though they had no additional errors circled or marked. She gave a *tisk* noise with her mouth and turned away, not saying another word. I put my head in my hands. *Please just send me back to Seattle.* At least there I know what the freaking expectations are.

Nash walked in a minute later, reaching my boss quicker than I could reach the doors, and I knew I was in for it. So, I did the only rational thing. I went straight to the stairs, down to the lobby, and out to the waiting car. If he was going to yell at me, he could do it at the house, not in front of people I'd have to see every day for the next three months.

Chapter 6

"All I needed you to do was *try*, Even." Nash was exhausted, I could tell. "Why couldn't you do that?"

"I did try, Nash!" I let out a painful laugh. "Did she not tell you the part where I read through the same documents *twice*, and still didn't find whatever issues she did?"

"They were all on the first page! The titles barely matched what was in them."

"I told you, I don't understand business jargon! And she said I was looking for grammatical errors not business title errors. I didn't even look at the titles. Besides, why give me work she already knows how to fix?"

"She was giving you a chance to prove yourself." He sighed, looking around the room, probably for a bottle of something brown.

"Prove myself." I scoffed. "Okay, I get it. I'm a fuck-up. Send me back to Seattle, I can rot in jail all summer. Then you won't have to worry about me tarnishing your precious image."

He winced. "It's not my image I'm worried about."

"I just don't get what I'm doing here, Nash!" I yelled. "I'm completely useless."

"We are here to take care of people," he said calmly—too calmly. He was so different since the plane. I hated it.

"The only person I need to take care of is myself, you taught me that."

"That's not a good mindset, Even. I know that now. We have the potential to make a difference—to really take care of people."

"Oh, like you take care of me?" I scoffed.

He sighed. "I'm trying here, Ev. I really am."

"When you spend more nights in your own bed than you do on a pull-out couch at the office, then I'll believe you're trying."

I turned toward the door, feeling him eye me as I went. This whole trip was a bad idea. He should have just let me rot in juvi. Hell, he should have just let me go to foster care. I'm sure he'd be much happier. And there was a chance so would I.

"Where are you going?" he asked, as I reached the front door.

"I just need some air, is that okay?"

"I'm sorry," he muttered, halfway under his breath.

"For what?" I asked, pausing in the doorway.

42

He looked up, surprised. "Not being there when I should have been."

I swallowed hard, closing the door behind me. I was not going to feel guilty for him not being there for me. I was not. That was on him. That was his problem. Still, there was a knot in my throat because he was the only family I had, and I wanted him to love me. Shit, I just wanted someone to love me.

Once outside, I reached into my jacket pocket, pulled out a pack of cigarettes, and stormed off as far from the house as I could.

Shit, it was beautiful here. The house Nash had rented for the summer backed up to the Grand Parc Miribel Jonage. It was a nature reserve, which I only knew because I could see the sign as I made my way around the pool and through the back yard.

⚮

The sun was setting as I made my way to the park. I wasn't sure what the restrictions were. Parks in Seattle close when it gets dark, but only riff raff like me were brave enough to go anyway. Brave enough? Stupid enough? Did it matter?

At least I had the excuse that I wasn't from around here. Though, with Nash being so stern about going to jail if I got in trouble, I had a feeling that wouldn't save me all that much. He was probably just waiting for the opportunity. He'd probably get more work done without me around.

It wasn't long before I was in the woods, on a trail, walking aimlessly. I was probably going to get lost, which was fine by me. It's not like anyone would really miss me, anyway. Only it was pretty dark in the woods now, and that felt eerie, even to a trouble maker like myself.

I was a trouble-maker, not a ghost chaser.

I was just about to turn back when I saw it; the same glowing orb from my dream was dancing about only a few feet from the trail. I don't know how I knew it was the same orb, but I *knew.*

My feet were leading me off the trail before I could think better of it, and I should have. Dream orb hadn't seemed all that nice.

It was floating near the base of a tree. I could almost see the outline of—something in all that light when I heard a crack, and the earth beneath my feet gave way.

Chapter 7

I was falling down a hole that felt endless. I'd given up screaming, and I'd started reaching for anything I could instead. My hands caught on three different books, a tea-pot, and a basket full of apples before I started pinching myself. I reached out for a rope, but I'd only just caught my grip when I realized it was human hair and quickly let go. I grabbed onto a vine, but the pumpkin on the end gave way with me, bouncing against the wall and bursting, leaving me covered in seeds. The air had a hint of salt as I reached out and nearly got snagged on a fishing net. But it was when I caught a lit candelabra that yelled at me that I knew I was dreaming.

Another shriek escaped my lips as I reached for the walls of this never-ending hole that seemed to be caving in on me, but all I could feel were loose rocks. I must have pulled one too many, because once the hole began to curve, an avalanche of rocks came tumbling after me.

I crashed into a cold stone wall, and I'd only just let out a groan when the loose rocks came crashing into the entry-way of the hole, leaving me trapped in a tiny space, barely big enough to breathe.

I instantly felt myself swell with panic. I was going to die, and no one would even know where to start looking. And, sure, that sounded alright when I was down in the dumps, but I still had survival instincts. Why was I so stupid? Sure, Even, just walk off into the woods and go off-trail after a floating orb from your dream. That's brilliant.

I tried to focus my breathing, trying to ground myself. It was dark, but I could feel four walls all around me. My heart began to race. I felt my breath quicken, and for a moment, I was back in my parents' car. My eyes started to swell, and I tried slowing my breathing again, but I felt like it wouldn't be long before I ran out of air.

I tried to count to ten. I only got to three before I stuttered and had to start over. I tried grounding again, because that always worked. Only it didn't. It was too dark to see anything. There was absolutely no grounding my way out of this one.

I kicked at the rocks as best I could, but they wouldn't budge.

I needed light. Wait, I had my stupid phone. I squirmed, struggling to reach for it in my back pocket. Of course, I had no signal. Perfect. At least the battery was still almost full. Wasn't like I could do much with the damn thing to drain it down.

My vision was going black from all the breathing, but I tried to use the light anyway. How was I getting out of here? A door! There was a tiny door just big enough for my shoulders to fit through. I pushed on it, and it gave way with a rather loud creak, but the moment I slipped through onto the stairs outside of it, I could breathe again.

⊗⊗⊗

I lay on the cobblestone steps for what felt like an eternity before I could breathe normally. My heart rate slowed down to a normal level, and I finally stopped shaking. Once I felt okay again, I knew I had to get up and get the hell out of here. I knew what was behind me, so the only way out was up.

The stairs ascended for what felt like forever, winding until I felt like I had to be touching the clouds. There weren't any windows just an endless spiral of cobblestone that led up and up and up. I couldn't see down, which meant my options for getting out of here were dwindling by the minute. But I kept going. There had to be something up there.

My legs ached by the time I reached an old, worn wooden door, similar to the one down below, but fit for the size of a human rather than a dog. I eyed it for a moment. There was a chance it was locked. That thought made my heart sink. I took a deep breath and pushed. It gave way with a *whoosh* as it opened, kicking up a gust of dust. It almost felt like I'd opened an airtight seal.

Inside was a simple but large bedroom from what I could see with the little light that came through the boarded window. An armoire sat across from an oversized bed. The canopy bed was made of beautiful twisted branches, covered with a sheer, white material, that was also covered in a thick layer of dust.

I made my way around the room, kicking up clouds with my sneakers, as I reached the armoire. Atop it was a silver-handled mirror, a brush, and a book. All of them were coated in dust as well. The cover of the book was so coated that I couldn't see the title, and without thinking better of it I picked it up.

47

What I expected to be some sort of novel was actually more of a journal. The writing was in French, and I could barely read some of the words as some of the phrases were older, from another time. People just didn't talk like that anymore, but I found it interesting anyway as I leafed through the pages. My curiosity was spiraling as I flipped carefully through the old delicate sheets, scanning for anything that made sense.

My eyes fell upon a name that made me freeze and the book slipped from my hands.

Aurora.

This was a joke. It had to be a joke. No, I was dreaming. That's all. I leaned down to pick up the book, and heard something, twisting for the sound of it—the sound of...breathing.

Impossible, I knew that, but as I found myself holding my own shaking breath, I heard it again. I set the book down and slowly made my way toward the shrouded bed. Upon closer inspection, I realized it was occupied.

My heart began to thunder again as I inched closer, shaking more with each step. The figure came into view more the closer I came, a small figure in the middle of the bed, saved from the dust only because of the thin woven fabric draping over the canopy.

I moved the sheer fabric only slightly and sucked in a quick breath of air.

In my life, I'd never accepted the possibility of true love, love at first sight, or soulmates. Nothing was *meant to be.* Our existence was but a blink in the life of time. We were simply happenstance. And for so long I'd denied the possibility that anything was perfect. Everything had flaws.

She did not.

This soft-skinned being, whose face looked like it might have been sculpted from clay, a work of art that would have taken a lifetime. Her hair cascaded down the pillow in strands that someone could have told me were made of real gold and I would have believed them. Each breath she took felt like it came from my own lungs, and it challenged every belief I had. Because despite myself, the moment I saw the rose in her cheeks, the only word I could find for my feelings of her was *love.*

Every fiber in my being was urging me forward, giving me no ability to ask why. My brain, out of sorts as it was, told me to kiss her, wake her, love her. Though my breath was still shaky, there was a part of me that could not stop myself as I leaned forward to her—no I was being pulled to her instinctively by a desire I didn't quite understand until my lips met hers. Because as I looked at her, I knew her.

I'm not sure what I expected as a gust of wind washed over us. It sent most of the dust from the room, knocking down the boards on the window, and let in a light that illuminated the space so clearly that I could see every shade of blue in her diamond eyes. Her skin glowed as her eyes met mine, a familiarity washing over them. And then she shrieked.

I jumped back at the sound, falling onto the floor hard. A groan escaped my lips. She backed up all the way to the wall, pulling her feet underneath herself as she shouted to me in incomprehensible French that sounded *old.* Her hands were ushering toward the door, which was my only real indicator of what she was saying.

"Oh, shit." I stammered, trying to get on my feet without scaring her. "Of course...Of course you speak French. That would be my luck. Ummm. Aurora?"

She locked eyes with me. I let out a breath.

"Okay, um…" I would struggle remembering every single word of French I'd ever been taught.

"You speak English," she breathed. The words were somewhat broken, but they made sense.

"*You* speak English!"

"I speak six languages." Her eyebrow raised like she was trying to be intimidating, but really it was just cute. "Now, you leave or I call the guard."

I swallowed hard. How was I supposed to tell her there wasn't a guard? No king or queen. No kingdom. France had a president now. Her family was gone. Everything she knew was changed. Unless she wasn't really a few hundred-year-old princess who'd been waiting all this time for my kiss. There was still a chance this was all just a dream.

"Are you really Aurora?" I asked. "Like, *the* Princess Aurora?"

"But of course. And *who* are *you*?"

"I'm…just Even." I shrugged, as she eyed me with a sharp glare.

I let out a breath and bit my lip. How was I supposed to tell her?

"*Garde!*" She yelled, eyeing me when there was no response.

"Aurora," I breathed. "There's no guard."

"What have you done?"

"It wasn't me. It was just…" She was frowning at me. God, she looked angry, scared maybe. I wasn't sure. "Time, I guess."

Her frown deepened.

"You've been asleep for a very long time." I said slowly. "A very, very long time."

"I do not understand."

I took a step toward her, and she shrunk back further, so I stopped. My hands were shaking. God, she looked so much like that girl from my dream. That was so stupid. That was a dream. It wasn't real. But neither was the fairytale, yet here I was talking with a few centuries old princess.

No, I wasn't. I was going to wake up any minute now. It didn't feel like a dream, though.

"You were cursed… I think." I shrugged. "Your story is a fairytale now—a bedtime story for children."

She was shaking her head when she rose from the bed and rushed to the window.

"Wait—"

"Oh," she breathed, looking out at the dark forest, only illuminated by the moonlight, which was abnormally bright. You couldn't see much, but it was clear she couldn't see what she'd expected to.

When she turned back toward me, there were tears in her eyes, like she finally understood what I'd been trying to say. I was not the right person for this. I wasn't good with people. I was a loner stoner. And then, she started breathing heavily, a feeling I knew all too well, and I went to her.

She didn't stop me this time as I took her arms in mine.

"Hey," I said softly, "Listen, what do you see?"

She shook her head, her breath getting quicker. I almost thought she'd just shake me off and let the panic consume her.

"Look around, what do you see?"

"My room." She shook her head again, her breath growing quicker as her eyes started to swell with tears.

"What else?" I whispered, trying to look into her eyes.

"My…armoire."

I nodded. "What do you feel?"

"Your… hands," she said, still not meeting my eyes.

"What can you hear?" I asked.

"Birds."

"What can you smell?"

"The dust," she muttered, and I could feel her calming finally.

"And can you taste anything?"

Her stomach gave a growl. That was probably a no. She shook her head.

"Are you alright?" I asked.

She nodded, then promptly shook her head before falling into my arms and crying. They were heavy sobs that shook us both and made me want to cry with her. But I didn't say anything. I didn't move, I didn't pull away. I just held her, let her cry, and did whatever she needed right then. I didn't even know why.

Chapter 8

I've never been good at sorting out my own problems. Obviously, since I get high or drunk to numb my own traumatic memories and get into trouble to get my uncle's attention. So, why I thought for even a second I'd be able to help her with hers was beyond me, but I was going to try regardless.

It was getting late when Aurora finally calmed down enough to pull herself away from me again. And she did pull away, halfway across the room and far from my reach. I guess that was just as well. She didn't know me, even if I was so sure I knew her.

I hated that she was afraid of me—hated that she was afraid of anything. I hated that I was still in this dream. When was I going to wake up already?

I'd only just had this thought when I felt the ground begin to shake. I'd only ever felt small earthquakes, but they were enough to know we weren't safe in this old tower. And with every second, it was getting worse.

Aurora looked to me, panicked.

"We have to go," I called, rushing to the window. There was no way we were making to the ground by stairs.

It wasn't that far of a jump. I hoped.

"No." She shook her head furiously, cowering further into the corner.

"You can't stay here. At least let me get you somewhere safe."

Small pieces of stone began falling from the ceiling, one landing just shy of her shoulder, and she jumped from the floor. She raced across the room to me, grabbing the book. No, she wasn't coming for me, just for the book.

She turned back toward the door where I'd entered, and a beam from the ceiling came down, blocking it entirely. She shrieked before she finally ran to me.

"What do we do?" She asked, not meeting my eyes as she scanned the darkness outside.

"Jump," I breathed.

She looked up at me with wide eyes, shaking her head furiously. I think we both knew it wasn't safe inside anymore, but she was clearly scared.

I took her shoulders in my hands. "You can do this, okay?"

She shook her head again, but another beam fell, then she nodded. So much doubt in those eyes. How I wished we could start over.

I didn't say that. Instead, I counted down "One, two, three!"

I am not normally a believer in magic, but when we reached the bottom of the tower, I was not expecting the walking trail I'd been on what felt like hours earlier to greet us. I guess at that point, I should have started believing in magic. All things considered, there wasn't a more logical explanation.

I looked up, and I could no longer see the tower window hidden amongst the darkness of the trees. And when I looked at Aurora, I realized she was looking up at it, too.

Aurora stiffened, clutching my arm. I wasn't sure what this used to be, all this forest around us. A castle? A kingdom? Maybe it meant something to her, but I didn't have the heart to ask.

"I'm sorry," I said softly.

The words had only just escaped my lips when I heard voices. Flashlights danced across the trail to our right, and in the beam, I could only just make out the shine of a badge. I knew what those looked like anywhere.

I jumped to my feet. "We can't...we can't stay here."

She nodded as I pulled her onto her feet and into the woods, away from the walking trail, which was my only clue about how to get back to the house. I held tight to Aurora's sleeve, tugging her along as I tried to avoid the beam of the security's flashlight.

We weren't exactly quiet. I heard a shout in French and footsteps following. My heart was pounding, and not just from the run.

"Who are they?" she asked as we ducked behind a tree, and I clamped a hand over her mouth.

"They're security guards," I hissed. "I think. Be quiet. If they see us, I'm dead meat."

"But they're the guard, they can take me to—" At least she was whispering.

"No, they can't."

She gave me a stern frown, and I huffed.

"Look, I'm trying to help you here, but if you want to go reveal yourself to a police -figure in the middle of the night with no ID and a backstory out of a young adult novel, be my guest."

"You're trying to help me."

It wasn't a question.

"Yeah, for reasons unbeknownst to me." I squeezed the bridge of my nose. "You don't have to come with me if you don't want to, okay? But…I'm not a bad enough person to just leave you out here. So, at least let me get you safe, fed—" I looked at her dirty dress. "Clothed? After that, you can decide what you want to do, sound good?"

She let out a soft breath and nodded. I could see the light beam retreating back toward the walking trail, away from us. They must have given up.

"Okay, I think the coast is clear, and by some miracle I actually know where we are. So, we're close. One last run?"

My phone buzzed as Aurora and I reached the house. Nash was headed to a dinner meeting with Autumn.

"Don't wait up," he said.

At the very least, I didn't have to explain Aurora to Nash—yet.

Aurora followed me inside almost silently. Her eyes danced around the tiny galley kitchen, and settled on minor details of the workings. Her gaze had only just made its way back to me when she let out a tired sigh.

"Hungry?" I asked, and her eyes lit up. "I'll take that as a yes."

I felt a laugh escape my lips as I started digging in the cabinets and tiny pantry. There wasn't a lot, but one thing was clear; Autumn had been there. I had a feeling pancake mix was not exactly a French staple. Autumn did know that it was one of the few things I could cook for myself.

"Breakfast for dinner." I smiled.

Aurora looked blankly at the box, then up at me with a puzzled expression.

I opened my mouth to explain and quickly changed my mind. "Why don't you just take a shower, and I'll get dinner started."

I led Aurora out of the tiny kitchen and into the equally tiny bathroom. Her eyes widened when I flipped on the light, and I was reminded that I'd have to catch her up on things like electricity. If she stayed, that was.

No, she wasn't staying. She was just getting settled until she could go…somewhere else—anywhere else. So long as I didn't have to explain her to Nash. Talk spreadsheets with that man all day, sure, but there's no telling him a fairytale princess was awoken by his niece in a tower in the woods.

I reached into the cabinet above the toilet and pulled out a towel.

"Here," I sighed. "You can get cleaned up in here. I don't really know what the water heater is like, so don't spend...so..."

Aurora was looking at me like I wasn't speaking English. Then again, it wasn't like English was her first language, anyway. Either way, she had no clue what I was talking about.

I stepped around her and turned on the shower. Her eyes widened and she peered into the shower, scanning it.

"You control the rain?" She looked at me like I was a witch. I mean, I did sort of dress like one sometimes. "Magic."

I choked on a laugh. "No, it's science."

She nodded, but I could tell she was not convinced. Then she let out a quick breath and held her arms out wide.

"You may undress me now." She said matter-of-factly.

At least ask me on a date first. "Oh, no. You're going to have to learn to tackle that on your own. I have dinner to cook."

Her arms fell flat, and she frowned like I'd deeply offended her.

"Don't look at me like that."

"But how will I—"

"Look," I sighed. "I'm not a...a dressing maid, okay? And you better hurry because I really don't know how long that water will be hot."

I heard a huff as I slipped out of the room and shut the door behind me.

I'd nearly finished dinner when Aurora began shouting my name at the top of her lungs.

"What?" I called down the hall, stopping dead in my tracks in the bathroom doorway to cover my eyes. She was naked. "Why—why—why are you shouting?"

"There's no bell," she replied innocently, waving around the room.

The fan was on, the toilet freshly flushed, still running, and the sink was going full blast like she might have tried every switch in the room looking for some kind of butler's bell to ring.

"What should I wear?" she asked finally.

I let out a sigh but refrained from reminding her that I wasn't a maid or a servant, because the truth of the matter was, she wasn't raised to do things herself. Instead, I darted into my room and grabbed a pair of shorts and a t-shirt from the suitcase Nash had packed. At least someone could get use out of them. They were way to tiny for me.

I set the clothes on the counter of the bathroom, trying to avoid looking at her, while I shut the door. My hand was still on the doorknob when she piped up again.

"What is this?" She huffed. "These are the shortest—*trousers?* I cannot possibly—"

I suppressed a laugh. "They're called shorts. You're in the 21st century now, no one cares if you show a little leg. Besides, no one's here but me, and you clearly don't care if I see you stark naked. You better hurry. Dinner's getting cold."

Aurora stumbled a couple times, making a loud thud against the wall. I thought about checking on her, but she didn't say anything. Maybe she'd never had to put on underwear before for all I knew. She was in the kitchen with my shorts on backwards a few minutes later.

I set a plate of pancakes down in front of us both and sat down. She eyed the table for a moment before clumsily pulling out her chair. I wondered how many things she was suddenly about to be forced to do for herself that she'd never done before.

"Thank you," Aurora said softly, but she didn't look up.

"You're welcome," I sighed, stuffing a bite of pancake into my mouth.

She grabbed the fork carefully and looked around for a moment before looking up at me. Her mouth opened, then shut firmly again.

"Something wrong?" I asked.

"This simply is not how you set a table. I—could I have a knife, please?"

I grinned, getting up and grabbing a butter knife from the silverware drawer.

"Thank you."

She took the knife and began carefully cutting the pancakes into the tiniest bites I'd ever seen. She chewed slowly, precisely. Shit, she must have thought I was some wild animal. I was halfway done already.

"You know—" I started, but I let out a breath and shook my head. She didn't need to know that being overly ladylike wasn't necessary. I had a feeling that being ladylike just might be all she had right now, and who was I to take that away?

"What is it?" She asked after she'd carefully chewed her miniscule bite.

"Nothing." I smiled. "Never mind, it wasn't important."

She nodded, and we finished eating in silence. Or, rather, I finished eating, and left her to her tiny bites to wash up the kitchen and try to make it look like only one person was eating dinner here rather than two.

I'd explain things to Nash eventually, maybe. I was hoping I wouldn't have to. I mean, she wasn't interested in sticking around. She wanted to stay somewhere else. I was just a stepping stone, right? Maybe I could get her on her way before Nash even knew she was here.

She nearly dropped the plate trying to get up and bring it to me. I wasn't sure if she was clumsy naturally or just because she was trying to do things she'd never before had to do. Either way, her frustration about it was kind of adorable. But I wasn't about to say so.

I put away the dishes and led Aurora down the hall to the room where she'd be sleeping.

"Listen," I sighed. "My uncle... He can't know you're here, okay? It's a lot to explain, but I'm already in trouble with him. So, just... be quiet, as best you can?"

Aurora nodded, clinging to the book she'd brought back from the tower. I wondered what she'd think if she knew I'd looked inside. I hadn't meant to pry into someone else's stuff. That is, I didn't figure after all that time that anyone alive would mind.

"I'll, uh," I let out a nervous breath, "I'll see you in the morning?"

"Yes, sleep well." She smiled. It was forced, almost pained, but I had a feeling that for now, that was the most I was going to get.

"You, too."

I slipped out and shut the door behind me. What was I doing?

"Hey," Nash said from my doorway.

"Hey," I said back, not looking up from my sketchbook. "How was dinner with Autumn?"

"Oh, um. Good. Just a business dinner, you know."

"Mhmm."

"So," he sighed. "I know where you were earlier."

I felt the blood run from my face.

"It's fine," he continued, "It's beautiful here, that's why I chose this place instead of a hotel. I thought… I thought maybe you'd draw or something instead of going bored out of your mind like you do in the penthouse."

I set my sketchbook down and looked up at him. I instinctively raised an eyebrow. He did something for me for once?

"Okay, okay, Autumn, suggested that it would be better for you."

A laugh slipped out my lips as I looked back down at my notebook. "Of course, she did."

He let out a sigh. "Listen, I don't think it's safe for you to be crossing that major highway like that, so I've taken the liberty of getting your own driver for the summer."

I looked up at him again. "But I thought—"

"I will still be keeping an eye on you. It's not like you'll be allowed to do whatever you want, and it won't be Gordon, so you won't be able to 'pretty please' your way about the city. But Autumn thinks, and I agree, that forcing you to wait until my work-day is finished might be a bit much."

"So you're going to be working longer days again?" My eyes began to swell, so I gritted my teeth and looked down. Two days in, and he's already going to be sleeping at the office.

"No, not like that." He let out a breath. "But there may be a day or two when I stay a bit longer. Punishment or not, you're... you're still a kid."

I met his eyes. He was different. Ever since the plane. Or maybe it was Autumn. Or maybe it was Autumn seeing me on the plane. I couldn't decide if I wanted to hug him or punch him, so I grabbed my sketchbook again instead.

"Thanks, Nash," I said, twirling my pencil in my hand.

"I'm headed to bed. You probably should be, too."

Chapter 9

I barely slept that night, though I tried really hard. My mind raced from the same old nightmares early in the morning. And while staring at the ceiling for the better part of an hour just day dreaming about seeing Aurora for the first time was nice, once I was awake, I was awake.

And day-dreaming about Aurora reminded me that there was a very good chance I'd dreamed the whole day before, and she wasn't asleep in our spare room.

That thought haunted me until I couldn't bear the thought of going back to sleep. I got up, got dressed, and crept into the hallway. The door to Nash's room was still closed, and I couldn't hear him bustling about yet, so I poked my head into the spare room as quietly as I could.

I could see a figure lying in the bed from the doorway, so I closed the door and let out a sigh. I had not dreamed the day before. I really had woken Sleeping Beauty. I wasn't sure if I was relieved or more anxious.

With no one awake, I slipped into the kitchen and got to work. I was fixing breakfast and coffee for me and Aurora, completely zoned out, unfazed as I hummed along. Why was I humming that song from *Sleeping Beauty*?

"What are you doing?" Nash asked, and I nearly jumped out of my skin.

"Just breakfasting—making breakfast," I sputtered, whirling around.

"You're cooking?"

"Yeah... This one's for... you."

"You made me breakfast?" He raised an eyebrow.

"Mhmm." I smiled.

"That's... sweetly out of character."

"You've just been so understanding about my behavior this summer, so I wanted to thank you." I smiled. "With breakfast."

"I don't know what you want, Ev, but if it's reasonable," he said, taking a bite of one of the tarts I'd found in the pantry. "I'm sure I would have considered it without a breakfast bribe."

"I don't want anything." *Besides you leaving.* "Honest."

He nodded slowly, took the tart with him and backed out of the kitchen. I let out a breath.

"Don't be late for work!" he called from the door, then he was gone.

Once the front door shut, Aurora poked her head in the kitchen. Her hair was sticking out in all directions. It was naturally that curly. Shit, she looked cute in my clothes.

No, Even. You are not allowed to think that.

65

"Did he leave?" she asked, tentatively.

I nodded.

"You look... fancy."

I let out a laugh. I assumed business slacks were much better than the dirty ripped jeans I'd been wearing the day before. "It's for work."

"Work?" She frowned.

"Yeah, these days people have these things called jobs where they trade labor for money."

She nodded slowly. "Do I have work?"

"No." I smiled. "At least not for now. You can just stay here, watch some TV... or something."

She blinked at me. I was going to have to explain television. How was this girl supposed to survive the 21st century?

"Here, have some breakfast." I smiled, handing her what would have been my plate. I turned back toward the cabinet and started more.

"How long will you be gone?"

"A few hours." I shrugged. "Don't worry, I'll turn on the history channel, and maybe you'll get caught up."

She stared blankly at me for a moment before I led her to the living room and turned on the TV. Her eyes widened in the same way they had when I'd turned on the shower. She had that 'first time seeing a magician' look in her eye.

"Here," I sighed, smiling as I put the remote in her hands. "These two buttons change the channels, so you can figure out what you like, I guess."

Aurora stared at the remote for a second before pushing one of the buttons. She jumped when the screen changed, but pushed the button again rather quickly, giggling to herself.

"You have fun with that," I laughed, grabbing my cup of coffee and chugging what was left as I headed back to the kitchen. "I gotta go. Stay away from the windows please!"

She didn't respond. Instead, she kept giggling as she changed the channel some more.

"Aurora!" I laughed as she jumped, turning to face me. "Stay away from the windows. Don't go outside. You might get lost."

"I wouldn't—"

"It's different than how you remember it, okay?"

She let out a sigh and nodded before taking a tentative seat on the sofa.

That was how I left her.

I slipped out of the house and out to the front entrance where my new driver was waiting. That was awfully fast.

"Good morning, Miss McCoy." He nodded. "I'm Henry, I'll be your driver."

I sighed, offering my best smile. "Can you call me Even?"

"Whatever you'd like, Even." He smiled back, opening the back door for me.

I wish I'd been focused enough to smile back, be a considerate human. But I couldn't stop thinking about Aurora being all alone in the house all day. It ate away at me the entire ride to work, but I didn't know why. Why was I worried about Aurora? I was just letting her stay until we found somewhere else for her. Why did I care?

I let out a sigh as we pulled in front of McCoy Enterprises. No more time to think about it.

⚬⚬⚬

Like the day before, my boss was in the center of the room, constantly reading this or that, barking orders, talking through a wireless phone, or on occasion, going to someone's desk to view their work. I headed straight to the desk where she'd sat me the day before, but I was caught halfway there by a woman Autumn's age.

"It's Even, right?" she asked, flashing a straight, white-toothed smile. "I'm Elaine."

Elaine was perfect in that high-profile sort of way. Solid cheekbones, flawless skin, an hourglass figure that she showed off in her high-waisted pencil skirt. And since she was the first person at the Lyon branch to seem happy to see me, she had kindness going for her, too.

"Nice to meet you." I smiled, taking the hand she outstretched. I hated handshakes, touching other people's hands, no thank you. "What can I do for you?"

"Well, I'm the head of the committee overseeing this summer's gala, and I was hoping—"

"The gala?" Madame Caron let out a hearty but icy laugh. "Miss McCoy can't even edit a simple document. You'd have better help if you passed flyers out on the street."

My cheeks burned, and I felt my eyes begin to swell, but I blinked it back. I would not give her the satisfaction of seeing me cry.

"Sorry," I smiled to Elaine. "She's right, I'm really not qualified. I'm sure there are plenty of interns here who could be of more help."

"But Mr. McCoy said—" Elaine began.

"I'm sure Mr. McCoy was only talking her up." Madam Caron waved Elaine off. "After all, that is why she is here in the first place."

I sucked in a pained breath and headed toward my desk again only to find all the documents were gone. The desk was empty. Shit.

"*Mademoiselle* McCoy." I heard her sharp voice sing behind me. I was suddenly terrified of what she'd be having me to that day.

"Madame." I said, turning with a forced smile.

"I have found something more suited to your skillset." She said, taking a slip of paper from her assistant, who I then realized was standing behind her. "We have a… board meeting at ten. I trust you can manage getting coffee?"

"Of course." Finally, something an intern is supposed to do. How I was supposed to find a coffee shop, I didn't know. But, with all the English speaking business people around here, there was at least a chance I could get the order right.

Wrong.

The page she handed me was handwritten in French. I could read a total of six words. I looked up at her and forced a smile. She was sneering. Why did she want me to fail so badly?

"I'll have them hot and ready at ten." I smiled. "Anything else I can do in the meantime?"

"Stay out of my way."

I let out a breath as she turned away from me. It was exactly 8:15. I had an hour and forty-five minutes to get coffee. That was literally my only job for the entire day. Maybe. I'm sure if I got it right, she'd find something ridiculous for me to do. But she was counting on me getting it wrong, which is why I left immediately, and found my driver still outside.

"Miss McCoy," he said with a polite smile. His accent was thick, I now noticed. He hadn't said much since I'd met him that morning. I missed Gordon. "Mr. McCoy insisted you stay at work until lunch."

"Leaving is part of work," I said, holding up the piece of paper my boss had given me. "I'm an intern. Gotta get coffee. Know anywhere good?"

"I might know a place." He nodded, handing the page back to me.

"Can we stop by a shop while we're at it?"

"I'm sure Mr. McCoy would be happy to get you whatever you need on his own time."

"I need a translation book," I said as I slid into the back seat, knowing full well Nash had told him not to take me anywhere that wasn't pre-approved. "Also for work."

He nodded, putting the car into drive and heading down the road.

I didn't always care. In fact, there wasn't a lot I cared about, but I'm a prideful little shit, and I know it. Not knowing how to read my boss's notes ground my gears. Having her talk down to me was even worse. I didn't think highly of myself. I didn't think because Nash was my uncle that somehow made me better than everyone else. But I was deserving of being treated with the same dignity as the rest of her employees.

I made it to the meeting at 9:58, slipped inside as they were about to start, passed around coffee, offering a caution *in*

French, and slipped back out. I ignored the raised eyebrows from Madame Caron and Nash, who was at the head of the table. I ignored my inability to understand the responses, and I ignored the other interns and assistants as I returned to my desk to do a whole lot of nothing the rest of the day.

Not only had I found a book to translate French, but I was able to find one of those computer programs that teaches it to you word by word, which I found very odd for a city *in France* to have, but I was stoked regardless. I'm sure learning French at my place of work, in France, wasn't the best timing, but it was all I had.

The thing was, I knew basic French. I could ask where the bathroom was, tell them I had an emergency, give my name, that sort of thing. I knew a lot more French than I'd realized when we arrived, but these were native French people. French was their *first* language, which meant, they spoke it ridiculously fast. It was the speed that I had trouble with.

I was going to use every minute I had in this stupid office building to not make a fool of myself.

I decided that while I was doing that, it was worth checking to see if Molly had finally gotten back to me. She hadn't. From what I could see on her account, she wasn't really all that active. Hell, maybe she'd finally gotten arrested, since she didn't have me getting caught for her.

I wrote another message, telling her about how awful the job was and how I wished I was home. I left out the part about Aurora. Left out the part about learning French. I left out a lot actually. I realized just after sending it that I had to censor the things I told my best friend. And that was sad.

"Aurora?" I called as I stepped into the house just after 5 PM.

The TV was still running something on the Discovery Channel. By some miracle there wasn't a fire or worse. But apart from the noise coming from the TV, the house was completely quiet.

My heart began to pound as I shut off the TV and headed down the hall to the spare bedroom. It was empty. Fuck.

For a moment my mind was racing, trying to think of all the places she could have gone. I slipped out of the room as I unbuttoned my silk button-down. No way was I searching this city in this outfit.

I had my shirt halfway off when I opened my door to find Aurora sitting on my bed. I'd never turned around so fast in my life.

"I'm sorry," she said quickly, looking down. "I didn't mean to—"

"What are you doing in here?" I asked as I reached into my suitcase for a t-shirt.

"I wish I knew," she mumbled. "The TV was so overwhelming, and I didn't know how to turn it off."

I wanted to be mad, but she looked scared when I turned back around. I let out a sigh and sat down on the bed next to her.

"Have you eaten anything?" I asked.

She shook her head. She still hadn't met my gaze. I felt my eyes narrow.

"Did something happen?"

"I—I might have looked in your book. I didn't know it was—I'm sorry."

I let out a laugh. "My sketchbook? I mean, it's okay, I guess." It wasn't. It felt like a major invasion of privacy, but I knew she hadn't meant for it to be.

"I closed it quickly," she mumbled. "Once I knew what it was. I was just…curious."

"What? About me?"

She nodded.

"Why?" I smiled. "I thought you just wanted to find some place—"

I heard the front door open and jumped to my feet.

"Ev, you here?" Nash called.

"Shit." I whispered. "Get in the closet!"

"What?" she asked, jerking away as I tried to pull her to her feet. "No!"

"Aurora, get in the damn closet, or we are both toast!"

"But—"

I could hear Nash's steps getting closer, so I grabbed her by the shoulders and began shoving. She wasn't fighting much, and I wasn't being rough, but she was very clear that this was not okay. I'd only just slammed the closet shut when Nash opened the door.

"Hey, didn't you hear me?" he asked. "Were you talking to someone?"

"Who, me?" I laughed, picking up a shirt out of my suitcase to busy myself. "Just to myself."

"Autumn wanted to know if you felt like joining us for dinner. There's apparently some place near the river she wants to try."

"Oh, yeah?" I grinned. "You two sure are spending a lot of time together outside of work."

He rolled his eyes. "I don't know how it's escaped you, but we spend a lot of time together regardless. Autumn doesn't have any friends here, Even. I do."

I nodded, but I was still smiling. He had no idea how badly Autumn had the hots for him. Completely oblivious. And it wasn't like she was a bad person. She was pretty great, actually.

"So, dinner?" he asked.

"I'm actually really tired." I sighed. "I kind of want to get unpacked since we'll be here a while. Maybe watch a movie or something."

"Okay," He forced a smile as he scanned the room. "Do you want me to bring anything back for you?"

"Umm. Surprise me."

"That's not dangerous at all."

I laughed as he stepped out.

"Behave!" he called behind him.

I let out a deep sigh, and Aurora threw open the closet door. There was fire in her eyes. Her hand flew at me, and I only had a split second to avoid a nice slap to the face.

"Whoa!" I said as she went for another one. I caught both her wrists. "Stop it!"

"How dare you! Just who do you think you are?" She was practically shrieking. "Let me go."

74

"Are you going to slap me?" I asked, still holding tight to her wrists.

She let out a huff, looking away, but she shook her head.

"Okay, then."

I let her wrists go, and she stomped toward the door, stopping before she stepped out.

"I'd like for you to find somewhere else for me to stay. This simply will not do."

Then she stormed off into the spare room, slamming the door behind her. I let out a sigh and fell onto my bed. I was in way over my head.

Aurora didn't come out for the rest of the night. She refused to join me for dinner, so I left a plate in front of the door. It was gone when I came back down the hallway after I was done.

I spent the rest of the night trying to find some place I could take her. Nash had left his laptop on the table. It wasn't like the man ever changed his password. The more he went out to dinner with Autumn, the later he came home, so I wasn't exactly worried about getting caught.

There weren't a lot of shelters in Lyon. Then again, I didn't want to drop her off at the doorstep of a homeless shelter. Not only was that dangerous, but it was counterintuitive. What was worse, most of them were full, anyway.

I started looking into a halfway house, which was probably her best bet. It wasn't like she was recovering from anything, not really. But she definitely needed help getting adjusted to the modern world.

By some miracle, I found one. I wrote down the address and took a crappy photo of the map with my phone before I headed to the spare room. I knocked.

"Hey."

"Go away," she called from inside.

"I found a place." I sighed. "I can take you tomorrow after work."

She was quiet for a moment. I let out a sigh and was about to head to my room when she opened the door.

"Tomorrow?" she asked.

I nodded. "We can go as soon as I get home, but we will have to walk because the driver Nash hired will one hundred percent rat me out."

"Alright." She nodded. "Here."

She grabbed the plate I'd left and handed it to me.

"Thanks." I smiled. "Aurora, I'm...I'm sorry about the whole closet thing. It's just—I can't get in trouble with Nash any more."

"Well, after tomorrow, you won't have to worry."

Her eyes met mine, and all the fear and pain in them made my chest ache.

Aurora was beautiful. The more I saw her face, the more I was certain she was that girl from my dream. She was the literal girl of my dreams. I'd woken her after who knows how long. I knew that meant something. It meant something more than I might ever comprehend. But it wasn't the right time. I was too young for soulmates and true love.

And I had a feeling no matter how much a part of me wanted to kiss her again, the feeling wasn't mutual.

"I'm sorry," I breathed, breaking the silence that had passed over us.

She nodded. "Me too."

There was a knock at my door that didn't wait for a response. Nash.

I looked up, and he let out a sigh. "Sorry, long meeting. Did you eat?"

"Yeah, I ate a while ago." I shrugged. There was a small box in his hands.

Nash nodded slowly, eyeing my bed, which was now strewn with notebooks, my sketchbook, and just outside my guitar case, a pack of cigarettes. Shit. Oh, shit, I was dead. Done for. Finished. I can come out now.

He took a breath like he might say something about it, then smiled at me. "I'll put this in the fridge. It should still be good tomorrow."

"Okay." I nodded as he slipped out the door. I fell back against my bed and let out a sigh of relief.

"You really should go to bed soon," I heard Nash call from the other side of the door.

He was right. It was inching on midnight. I started gathering up my stuff, and I heard another knock at the door.

"I'm going to bed, Nash," I groaned.

Rory poked in her head.

"Oh, hey, come in." I paused, ushering her quickly before Nash heard anything. "Everything okay?"

She nodded, stepping into the room and eyeing my guitar, the notebooks, my sketchbook. It was almost like the whole closet incident hadn't even happened.

"This is beautiful," she said, picking up my sketchbook.

I felt myself tense up. She knew what it was now.

"That's umm…" I breathed.

"I'm sorry," she stammered, quickly handing it back to me. "I didn't mean—"

"It's okay. It's just… showing people my art is like showing them my soul."

"I like that." She smiled. "You play the strings?"

"It's a guitar." I smiled. "But, yeah."

"Will you play for me sometime?"

I held onto the way she said *sometime*. Like she hadn't asked me to take her to stay somewhere else. Like I hadn't found a place. Like she wouldn't be gone tomorrow.

I nodded, swallowing hard. "Did you need anything? I thought you went to bed a while ago."

"I'm just… nervous." She looked down. "About tomorrow."

"You'd probably be crazy if you weren't."

She let out a soft sigh and sat down on my bed. "Do you think I'll ever feel… at home?"

I swallowed hard. *I don't even know what home is anymore.* "Of course."

She nodded, not satisfied. "What if I fail?"

"Fail what? Being a teenager? Building a life?"

She nodded again, looking rather serious.

"I don't..." I sighed. I hated lying. "I don't think it's as simple as try and fail. I think we just do our best, and life does the rest."

"Do you?"

"Do I—"

"Do you do your best?" she asked.

"I—no, I guess I really don't most of the time."

She put a hand on top of mine, and my stomach tied in knots. I wished there was a way to tell it to stop that.

"Maybe one day, you will."

She stood, her touch fading from my skin as she slipped out of the room.

Chapter 10

There was a slice of pie for me in the fridge the next morning, and I waited until Nash had left to share it with Aurora. She was in a much better mood.

"You still nervous?" I asked, surprised that she didn't mind eating out of the same container as I was.

"Not anymore. Should I be?" she asked. Her back was rigid, though.

"I don't know."

"I cannot sit and do nothing every day, so I must find my place. If this is how I do it, so be it."

I swallowed hard. Suddenly the pie tasted like ash.

"If you're not ready—"

"I am. I was ready to rule a kingdom after all."

"I guess that's true." I sighed. *What I wouldn't give for half your drive.*

⌘

Henry didn't say much on the ride to work, which made me miss Gordon again. He was always such a chatterbox when it was just the two of us. I was ignored as I walked into the doors of the office, my boss not even caring I was there. Until I reached my desk, I didn't know what I'd be doing all day, but there was a list. In *French.*

A soft laugh escaped my lips. Joke was on them. Reading French was easier than understanding spoken French. At least reading meant I could take my time. So I pulled out my book for the words that weren't familiar and got to work.

When I checked my social media account, Molly had finally messaged back. She was doing a cleanse. She said something about trying to stay away from social media. 'Sucks to suck on the dream summer vacation, and sure I miss you, but I'm too busy for your crap right now.'

'Miss you too.' I sent back. I considered sending more. Instead, I just went back to the list my boss had given me.

At lunch, I looked up the halfway house again and called their office number. I needed to double check they were accepting new people before I just showed up with Aurora.

"*Bonjour.*" A woman's voice chimed after the fourth ring.

"Hi, do you speak English?" I asked.

"Uh, yes? How can I help you?"

"Perfect, I'm looking for a place for a friend to stay until she can get back on her feet. She's not in trouble or anything, but she needs help finding work and getting settled."

"We do take non-criminals from time to time." She sighed like she was already tired of the conversation. "Under special circumstance. You can bring her by and my manager could speak to you."

"Great, yeah, we can come by today, if that's okay?"

"Yes, he will be here all day."

"Thank you!" I said, barely getting it out before I heard a click. "Have a good day," I mumbled to myself.

Most of the day was spent shredding documents, getting lunch for others in the office, or running errands for Elaine while Madam Caron was busy. I had a feeling I'd be doing a lot more work with her in the weeks to come, regardless of what Madam Caron said. I guess I didn't mind that so much. I was good at planning parties.

By the time I got off, I was so ready to get out of there. I had to get Aurora settled, and I knew it would take us forever to find the place, even with me looking at the maps the night before.

Aurora was waiting on the couch for me when I got home just after 5. Her back was straight, her legs crossed at the ankles, and her hands were in her lap, a confident stance, but she was shaking. She was also still wearing pajamas.

The thought hadn't occurred to me to suggest she raid my closet while she was being shoved in it.

"Let's get you changed," I sighed, leading her to my room.

I decided to change, too. I didn't feel like walking through the city in my business wear.

Autumn had insisted on my buying three dresses for work, for a change of pace from black slacks and blazers. I was not a dress kind of girl—hadn't been in years. The last time I'd worn a dress was the night my parents… anyway. There was no harm in giving them to Aurora. I had a feeling she'd be much more comfortable in them than a pair of my jeans.

"Here," I said as I stepped into the hall where Rory was standing, holding all three of them by the hangers. "You can wear whichever one you want."

She nodded, and I slipped into the spare room.

A part of me didn't want to do this—find her a different place to stay. I woke her, which meant in some freaky magical way that I had to be her true love or some nonsense, right? I didn't even believe in magic or true love. I should have just left her at the train station, handed her some cash, and wished her good luck. Someone would have helped her.

Or hurt her.

Damn it. I was only 17. I was not ready for a secret like this. I didn't like to lie. I hated to lie. But I had a feeling no one wouldn't listen. Not to the truth anyway. Without the truth, she was just a 16-year-old girl with no parents, no home, and nowhere to go. Sounded familiar.

I heard the door open and turned, my breath caught in my throat. I got that queasy feeling in my stomach that means you've probably eaten too much cheese, or seen the most beautiful human being on the planet eyeing you while wearing a red dress. Her cheeks flushed, and she smiled. I felt my heart pound a little and swallowed hard.

I was screwed.

"Even?" she asked. *Say it again. Or ten thousand times on loop.*

"Uh-huh?" I choked out.

"Can you help me? I don't know how to—" She turned around, her back exposed in the gap that a zipper should have closed.

Good God. I was not ready for this—this feeling as I closed the distance between us. The immediate knots that tied in my stomach as I brushed my hand against her skin. The shaking in my hands as I zipped the back of the dress, and the way she held her hair back with her hands as she looked over her shoulder.

Time was slow for a second as she turned back around letting her golden hair cascade to just below her chest. She was so close to me that I could almost feel her breath against my cheeks. She smiled again. I wished she'd stop doing that, but at the same time I wished she'd never stop.

"How do I look?"

"Won—per...um." I stammered and let out a deep breath. "Great, you look great."

She smiled again, this time a little more nervous, and looked down at her tiny feet where she'd slipped back on the same shoes I'd found her in. They were worn leather, just wrapped around her tiny feet. They'd have to do, though, because there was no way she could wear mine.

"You ready?" I asked.

She nodded, but her face didn't sell it. And I didn't know how to convince myself that I was doing the right thing.

The walk to the halfway house was long. I was glad I'd taken the photo of the map, or we would have gotten lost. Actually, I thought we were lost when we arrived.

It was less of a house and more of an apartment complex. There were two men standing outside writing down people's names as they came in, almost like a check-in. That was probably good for accountability. The two men looked up as we approached them.

"Hi, um," I let out a shaky breath. "Do you speak English?"

"Yes, we do." The taller of the two spoke up. He was the one holding the clip-board, taking down names. His friend didn't say anything.

"Awesome. I called earlier. Is your manager still here?"

"If there's something you need, we can help."

"Well, my friend," I pointed to Aurora, "She's needing a place to stay so she can get back on her feet. Somewhere she can start work, that sort of thing. I spoke to someone earlier and she said—"

"Does she have identification?" He sighed in that same way the girl on the phone had. Like he was tired of the conversation.

"Oh, um. No, she doesn't."

"I don't think we can help you."

"Listen, I was told to ask for the manager," I insisted. *Let me speak to your manager. Ugh I hated the sound of that.*

He let out another long sigh. "Name?"

"Aurora."

He raised an eyebrow. "Date of birth?"

I looked at Aurora who had been quiet the whole time.

"*Le 29 juin,*" Aurora said softly.

"She's 16," I added before they could ask.

Clipboard guy met my eyes.

"16?" he asked.

I nodded.

He shook his head and turned away, mumbling as he ducked inside. His friend stayed out, still quiet, which made me incredibly uncomfortable. Especially with the way he was eyeing Aurora. I was ready to leave. We should have just left right then.

"I thought you said they would let me stay," Aurora whispered with a shaky breath.

"Yeah, that's what I thought, too," I sighed.

Clip-board guy was gone for a long time. Aurora was getting impatient, and so was I. Finally, I heard his voice again from the doorway, calling to his friend. I groaned internally.

They talked in hushed tones for a minute before the word *police* rang in my ears, and I felt my blood run cold.

"Shit," I whispered, grabbing Aurora's hand. "We gotta go."

I pulled her around the corner where we'd come from, hearing a yell behind us. We'd only just rounded the corner, when I caught a glimpse of flashing lights, a sight I knew far too well for my own good.

"No, no, no, no, no," I called as I came sliding to a halt. Aurora crashed into me.

"Why are we running?" she asked, as I tugged her down an alley.

I heard a shout from the direction the lights had come, which made it clear they hadn't exactly missed us. The shouts grew louder, and suddenly they had flashlights on our back. I was regretting letting her wear a bright red dress now. They were hot on our tail, and Aurora was not the fastest runner. I was practically dragging her.

We ducked down every alley I could find. Left, right, left, right. It felt like we'd never get away from them. Until I yanked Aurora into a doorway, and we waited.

"What—" she started.

"Shhhhh, shh, shh, shh," I sputtered as I slammed a hand over her mouth. I wasn't rough about it, but it was firm.

The footsteps raced past the alley we'd ducked into growing distant by the second.

"Okay," I breathed, taking my hand off her mouth as I leaned ever so slightly out to look. I couldn't see any lights. "I think they're gone."

Aurora's hands grabbed my waist, pulling me back to her. I gasped, meeting her gaze.

"We should wait... a little longer." she whispered. "Just in case they come back."

I nodded. "Okay."

I was suddenly aware of just how tiny this doorway was, how close my face was to hers. I could feel her breath on my chest. But I was more aware of the fact that she still hadn't taken her hands off my waist. There was enough angsty energy in that tiny hole in the wall, I could have cut it with a knife.

The urge to kiss her washed over me. I wanted to, and by the look in her eyes, I wasn't convinced she'd stop me, but I knew better. I pulled away.

The walk back home felt longer than before. Maybe it was all the backtracking. Maybe it was that we kept ducking behind corners at every voice we heard. Or maybe it was just the disappointment, the nervousness, the feeling of the unknown pressing down on us both.

What was I supposed to do now? Tell Nash I'd woken Sleeping Beauty? Surprise! I found my soulmate in the woods! No way. And it wasn't like I could just send her packing either.

Nash sent a text when we were halfway home. *Late meeting tonight. I'll have something brought around for dinner.*

I wondered if his late meeting was with more people than Autumn, but I didn't ask.

Henry was waiting when we got back. He was on the phone. I felt my blood run cold. *Please don't rat me out. Please don't rat me out.*

"Oh, she's here," Henry said cheerily as he turned to me. "Some girl with her."

"Want me to talk to him?" I asked, hoping he'd say no.

"He asked where you've been."

"Just... sightseeing a little. It's France, after all."

"She said—yeah. Alright." Henry sighed. I got the feeling he hated this middle man nonsense. "He asked who your friend is."

"Prin—" Aurora began.

"Rory." I finished for her. "She's Rory. She's another intern."

Aurora looked at me questioningly, and I shook my head slowly.

"Thank you, Henry. Tell him to call me if he has anymore questions. I'm safe. I'm not in trouble. I didn't get arrested or hurt. I just listened to some street performers and got a coffee."

Henry nodded, still listening to Nash as he reached out a bag of food for me.

"Have a good night." I forced a smile.

I was dead. I was so, so dead. Nash was totally going to kill me.

"You can't just go running off without saying anything." Nash wasn't yelling. I could give him credit for that. "A text, Ev. That's all it takes. 'Hey me and another intern are going to get coffee.' Would that have been so hard?"

I swallowed hard. *Yes.* "No, I just… didn't think about it."

"Yeah, you didn't think. You're smarter than you give yourself credit for. You have got to start using that head of yours for more than mischief."

I let out a soft laugh.

"Oh, you think this is funny?" Nash asked, but he was smiling.

"Kind of." I grinned.

"It's not. I was worried about you. Just—" He let out a sigh. "It's my job to make sure you're safe, okay? And bad things happen to pretty girls in foreign countries, so don't go running off like that."

I nodded. All the humor had died from his voice. It was weird seeing him seem scared. It gave me chills.

"Can, um." I let out a breath. "Can Ar—Rory stay over?"

"Are you out of your—" He let out a breath. "You know what? Yeah, it's the weekend. I don't care."

"Really?" I raised an eyebrow.

"She seems like a nice kid." He rubbed his hands over his eyes. "Not the usual riff raff you bring around. Maybe she'll rub off on you."

I think she already had, but I wasn't about to tell Nash that.

"Thanks, Nash."

"Yeah, yeah." He sighed, waving me off. I heard him mumbling, "God, I need a drink," as I headed back to my room.

Aurora—Rory was sitting on my bed with her little book in her hands when I walked in. She looked up and smiled, closing it.

"He doesn't seem so mad."

"Yeah, that's because he doesn't know the truth." I laughed. "Whatcha working on?"

"Oh, it's nothing." She shook her head. "So, he said I could stay?"

"For tonight, I guess we will figure out the rest as we go."

She nodded slowly. "There's nowhere for me to go, is there?"

"Afraid not." I let out a long sigh as I sat down next to her. "Not unless I tell him the truth, or some variation of it. And I'm just not sure how to do that yet."

"I'm sorry for causing you so much trouble."

"It's not your fault. I'll figure it out, okay?"

"Maybe," she breathed, wringing her hands. "Maybe we can figure it out together."

"Yeah." I smiled. "Maybe."

Chapter 11

It was my first official weekend in France. Which meant McCoy Enterprises was closed for two whole days, following the flow of all its other branches. It also meant that Nash had no reason not to sleep in. And because I was a special kind of chaotic good, I slipped into his room and shut his phone off.

I jotted down the number for the house landline just in case, though I knew my phone wouldn't exactly call it. I'd find a pay phone. I'd seen one of those on our way back from the halfway house.

I tapped on the door of the spare room as quietly as I good. It was unlikely she'd hear me anyway.

"Hey," I whispered, cracking the door. "You awake?"

There was a beat, and for a short moment, I was convinced I was talking to myself.

"Yes." Aurora whispered back.

She was staring out the window, still draped in my pajamas. She didn't turn to look at me, and I wanted to ask what she was looking at, but I thought better of it. I knew what she was looking at—home. This place that she'd known so well long ago was now so very different.

"Why don't we get something to eat?" I asked, hoping to keep the mood light. "I can answer any questions you have. We don't have anywhere to be today."

She let out a sigh and turned around. Her eyes were sad, but she offered a smile and nodded.

Henry was waiting outside when we stepped out. I'd sent him a quick text when I'd woken up, hoping just maybe he would actually do what I wanted as well as Nash. I was surprised to find him waiting.

"Even, Rory." He smiled, nodding to us both. The guy didn't forget names, that was for sure.

Aurora tensed up next to me. I wasn't so sure she liked the nickname I'd given her. She mumbled a good morning to him as he held the door open for us, anyway. I had a feeling it wasn't him she was annoyed with.

"Why did you tell them my name was Rory?" she asked while Henry was heading around the car.

"Because Aurora isn't exactly a common name these days." I shrugged. "I was trying to help you blend in."

"Am I meant to blend in?"

Henry was in the car by now.

"I think that's impossible for you, but you can try."

"What do you mean?" She smiled.

"Some people are born to stand out." I shrugged, lowering my voice. "If you don't like it, I can tell them to call you Aurora instead."

"No, it's alright. I… I like it."

"Yeah?"

She nodded. "Rory it is."

Her eyes lit up as Henry started the car and pulled out. We passed by other cars and buildings at a relatively slow speed, but to her, we must have been flying. I had a feeling that horse-drawn carriages didn't get 35 mph.

"Where to, Even?" Henry asked from the front seat.

"Let's start with breakfast," I replied, "And maybe shoes."

Rory let out a soft laugh, looking down at her leather-clad feet. "Yeah, maybe shoes."

We started with breakfast of crepes and the strongest coffee I'd ever tasted at a tiny café near a shopping center. Rory's eyes were on everything, darting from one sound to the next, taking it all in. It was different in the daytime. I thought she might have sensory overload before we even finished our food. But the moment we'd finished and offered a quick goodbye to the café owners, she was practically dancing to the shopping mall.

It took nearly two hours for her to choose a pair of shoes safe for walking in, and I ended up buying her three. Actually, Nash ended up buying her three, but that wasn't the point. For some reason, watching her try on every pair of shoes in the store was more fun than I'd had all year.

By some miracle, Nash didn't mind that I was out exploring Lyon. So long as I stuck with my driver, who apparently doubled as a body guard. I was free to enjoy my Saturday. He'd somehow heard good things from my boss. I couldn't imagine how that was possible.

I took Rory everywhere I could possibly search for on the Internet. We visited the Museum of Cenema Miniature, which had teeny tiny versions of the coolest things. It also gave me the perfect opportunity to catch her up on world history, not that I was an expert. Still, she seemed to cling to every word I spoke, along with my hand as we walked through.

We went to the aquarium, which she found fascinating, La Basilique Notre Dame de Fourvière, and the Museum of Fine Arts, where she nearly got us arrested trying to touch one of the sculptures. That's the last thing I needed when Nash was so reluctantly trusting me with a day of freedom.

"Family heirloom." I shrugged to the member of security, pulling Rory away as quickly as possible as I tried to explain that we most definitely couldn't touch things even if she was 100 percent certain her father had *personally* commissioned it.

By the time we'd left the museum, it was inching toward evening, and we were both exhausted. She kicked off her shoes in the car and curled up next to me in the back seat. I let out a laugh. Had she chosen the best shoes for walking all day? No. Would I have convinced her to change them? Also no.

Rory drifted off to sleep as we rounded the block, her head resting on my shoulder. When I felt a buzz in my pocket, I had to carefully shift myself to get it out without waking her. I was grateful to Henry for his gentle driving as I read the message from Nash.

Headed to dinner with Autumn. Don't wait up.

I grinned. Autumn, again. And it was the weekend. No meetings. This had to be personal. I knew she'd been slowly falling in love with him for the better part of the last two years since I'd met her. She went above and beyond, and even I knew it wasn't because the pay was that awesome.

"Hey, Henry?" I said quietly, trying not to wake Rory.

"Yes, Mis—I mean, Even?" He said, eyeing me in the rearview only for a moment.

"Think we could stop and grab something to eat? Looks like Nash is headed out, and I don't feel like cooking."

Henry nodded, taking the next right.

Reluctantly, I woke her as we pulled up to the house.

"Hey," I whispered, "We're home. Are you hungry?"

She took a deep breath of air, blinking and nodded, making an agreeable 'mhmm' sound. I laughed.

"Come on." I smiled, taking her hand as I helped her stumble out of the car.

Henry trailed behind, having managed to grab the bags of things we'd bought while we were out.

"Thank you," I whispered to Henry as he shut the door behind us.

I started toward the spare room with the bags of things I'd bought for Rory while she took a seat on the couch and stared at a specific spot on the wall until I got back.

"Hey, you awake?" I laughed, still holding onto the bag of food Henry had grabbed us.

She jumped, but nodded as she turned to me.

"Let's go eat."

Rory was quiet as we sat down. She barely got out a thank you as I put a plate in front of her. I didn't hold it against her, though. It had been a pretty long day. Who knew you could see an entire city in one day?

I'd never been so content in silence. Normally, it was painful. I could hear everything in the nothing that other people could ignore. Something about silence with Rory was different.

She poked at her food for a while before she finally couldn't stop yawning long enough to chew, and I knew it was just time for bed. So, I put the food back in the containers it had come in, and set them in the fridge. Maybe we could snack on it the next day.

I walked her back to the spare room again in silence, bumping shoulders. When we reached the doorway, she paused there, looking up at me. She was smiling and blushing, and without saying a word she was saying so many things. I thought for one brief second she might kiss me before she turned and went to bed.

I let out a sigh and leaned against the wall. How was I in this deep so fast? And why was I just letting it happen when I knew it would only end in disaster?

Chapter 12

I woke to a gentle tap on the door. It wasn't Rory's knock, though.

"Hey, Ev," Nash called through the door. "I have some things I want to show you today. Wear something nice but comfortable."

Nice but comfortable. What did that even mean?

I rolled over and glanced at the alarm clock on the nightstand. At least he'd let me sleep in until 8. I sighed, rubbing my face before rolling out of bed and checking the closet I'd finally organized.

Business clothes, business clothes, too small clothes, and more business clothes. What was that he said I should wear? I let out a laugh before I put on a tight t-shirt and jeans. They didn't have holes in them, so that was nice, right?

When I stepped into the hallway, I could hear Nash's voice carrying in from the kitchen. I found him and Autumn sitting with coffee mugs in their hands chatting it up.

"Morning." I nodded, heading straight for the coffee pot.

I was glad Autumn was here because Nash absolutely could not make coffee.

"Did you have fun yesterday?" Nash asked as I poured sugar and creamer into my coffee. "Henry said you went to just about every tourist attraction on the map."

"Yeah." I nodded, taking a sip and letting out a sigh. "I really liked the art museum. You just don't see art like that anymore."

"Henry said you're getting close with... Rory? Is it?" Autumn asked. It was a loaded question. The most loaded of questions. A cannon, if you will.

"Yeah, she's really helping me with French, and...work stuff."

"Right." Autumn nodded, taking a long sip of her coffee. "Because she's an intern."

"Mhm." My throat was going dry despite holding a warm beverage in my hands. They might as well have put me in a dark room with a bright light shining on me. This felt like an interrogation.

"Did she stay over again last night?" Nash asked, but his tone wasn't the same as Autumn's. He was just asking. Nothing behind it.

"Yeah, we got in pretty late, so it didn't make sense not to. I didn't know we had plans today. Otherwise—"

"It's alright." Nash shrugged. "She can come along. I'm sure she'll find it interesting. Go see if she wants some coffee. I'd love to talk to her anyway."

Autumn and I locked eyes for a moment before I slipped out of the kitchen. When I turned back to look at her just before heading into the hall, she was still eyeing me. She knew. Shit, she knew.

⚬⚬⚬

Nash said we'd be exploring the city in a very different light. Along with Autumn, Nash felt I needed to see more of what the company does, why it's important, why I should care. One day it might matter to me.

One day, soon.

I didn't like the sound of that, but I went anyway, Rory in tow.

As Rory and I climbed out of the car to meet Nash and Autumn at one of the sites for the company, the realization that I knew little about McCoy Enterprises hit me. I knew we sold routers and stuff. We did IT. We did something with cybersecurity, but I didn't know much about that either.

But we weren't at McCoy Enterprises. Instead, we pulled up to a building much smaller than McCoy Enterprises that held multiple companies. I noticed on the elevator that each floor contained something different.

The four of us rode up to the fifth floor, which I was surprised to find was full of employees on a Sunday. They were all wearing McCoy badges, our logo in bold blue.

They were installing some wires, some hardware here and there, and a couple others were at the back talking with someone from the company based on the floor.

"So, they're just getting set up today." Nash beamed. "They're setting up an entirely new IT setup, using all McCoy products, so it will be built completely from the ground up."

I nodded, looking around at what looked like a mess, but everyone seemed to know what to do with it. I was not meant to install wiring apparently. I could barely keep my headphones from getting tangled. All that wire would have been in shambles on my watch.

Nash was still going on about the security we'd be installing later that day, and how our networking system would change the face of this startup in a day.

Rory was fascinated where I was bored, and Autumn, I think, only had eyes for Nash.

Maybe true love was real after all, and apparently it was unrequited.

"The great thing is that all of this hardware is recyclable!" Nash stated as he pointed toward some of the boxes they were wiring up. "Even the wire can be reused later on. And we've been working with hemp plastics lately as well."

Oh, yeah, because that's not hypocritical at all.

"Which is good because of the number of systems we install each year," Nash continued. "Approximately 60 percent of our overall revenue comes from system installations and upkeep. We would be nowhere without our IT department."

He had lost me. Once statistics came into play, I lost interest.

What did hold my interest was Rory, who seemed to hang on every word, and consider every number, as if she could do all the math in her head. The idea of energy was incredible to her. Computers were still this shiny new toy. How computers were entwined in our life was amazing to her. Seeing that light in her eyes was incredible to me.

We continued to meander around the floor, eyeing the work of the IT department as Nash kept up with the number talk. Then we went to another site, where the department was working on another system for a different type of company. Because of course we needed to see the different types of setups.

It was mid-afternoon before Nash decided to call it a day. We'd grabbed the briefest lunch possible between sites, and all of us were getting hungry again. Even Nash seemed to be hungry, and he forgot to eat half the time.

Neither Rory nor I felt up to a dinner out. Especially if it meant I had to dress up. But Nash wanted something specific, and Autumn was happy to go with him. I knew even before they were climbing into the car together and waving goodbye that something was up with them.

I just couldn't decide if I cared that much.

Rory and I decided to just go home and cook something. So far, Nash had kept the fridge pretty well stocked. I wasn't sure who was doing the shopping, though, as it clearly wasn't either of us. And I had only seen Autumn at the house once.

I had learned he'd found a housekeeper in France, as well. Never one to do his own laundry, I guess. A fact I'd learned only because while in France, I'd yet to do laundry, and somehow, it was always clean. I knew Rory hadn't learned how to use a washer and dryer yet.

When we walked in the door, Rory was still happy-go-lucky about the day we'd had with Nash, which was baffling to me. But listening to her talk about it made me smile as we checked the fridge for what we might be able to cook.

By the time we'd finished with dinner, I was tired, and while she didn't want to admit it, she was too. I cleaned up while she started eyeing the art hanging on the walls, and the book shelf in the living room.

"Even the piano has changed so much." Rory sighed, as I set the dishes aside to dry.

I'd been avoiding this piano. It was so nice in that vintage way that made every fiber of my classical-loving side *want* to play it.

"Well, people still play music from your time." I shrugged, not thinking as I spoke. "I had to study it when I was first learning to play."

"You play? Can you play something for me?"

I swallowed hard. "No, I don't really—"

"Please?" She had my hand in hers, which had my stomach in knots already, and I hadn't even sat down at the piano yet.

"It's been a long time," I breathed. I wasn't ready to talk about *why* I no longer play.

"Something simple, then."

"Rory…" I sighed.

"Please?" she asked again. It was her eyes looking into mine that did it.

"Okay, sure."

I'd been asked several times since losing my parents to play the piano. From parties to school functions by literally anyone knew who I'd played. The truth was that I'd tried, and when my fingers touched the keys, all I could think about was that night. That last hug from my dad. I knew they would have wanted me to keep playing, but I just couldn't.

Something about Rory made me want to be better, braver, stronger. I probably would have done anything she asked so long as she was saying 'please' while looking at me with those eyes.

I started off playing a song from Yiruma. It wasn't hard, and I knew Rory wouldn't know it, but she was in awe watching my fingers move across the keys. I was surprised at how much I remembered, not only of the song, but of the piano in general. Muscle memory was an amazing thing.

"That was beautiful." She smiled as I finished.

"Want to learn something?" I grinned, and she nodded.

It took me only five minutes to get her to memorize the simple half of the Heart and Soul Duet. It wasn't exactly hard, and she seemed to learn everything so easily.

"What's that one called?" she asked, grinning like she'd just won a first prize or something.

"It's called the Heart and Soul Duet."

She was so close to me, her hands having already brushed mine while playing. The way she was looking at me, her eyes were pulling me in, and it wasn't like I had to go far. Our faces were only inches apart.

"Should I play something else?" I whispered, just looking into her eyes.

She shook her head softly, her eyes not leaving mine.

I swallowed hard and leaned toward her. Our noses had only brushed when the front door opened, and I pulled away.

"Even, you're playing the piano?" Nash asked. He might not have even seen what almost happened from his tone.

"I asked her to." Rory smiled.

"And she agreed?"

I felt myself stiffen.

"She taught me something." Rory nodded.

"Did she now?" Now Nash was really interested.

"The Heart and Soul Duet," I said numbly.

"Oh, you used to love that one. Let's see it, then."

"I'm actually really tired," I said flatly and stood up.

Nash opened his mouth to speak, but I grabbed Rory's arm and dragged her to my room before he could say anything.

Maybe I should have taken it easy on Nash. It's not like him asking me to play the piano when I was already playing it was wrong. I just hated that it was expected. He didn't ask, not really. And it was like he'd been putting me in front of all these pianos, trying to force me back into it. Why didn't he get that I just couldn't love piano like I had before?

Nash knocked on my door an hour later. I'd apologized to Rory, she'd gone to bed, and I was deep in thought as I strummed through scales on my guitar.

"Hey," he said softly, letting out a sigh as I set my guitar to the side. "I wanted to check on you."

I raised an eyebrow.

"I shouldn't have asked about the piano. I know... I know that's hard for you."

"Then why do you keep bringing me around so many of them?"

He took a shallow, audible breath before stuffing his hands in his pockets.

"I didn't want you to give it up."

"I can still love music without playing the piano." I sighed, stuffing my music sheets back into my guitar case before slipping my guitar in, too.

"I know." He nodded. "You were really good, though, and I—"

"It's fine, Nash. Really. And it was nice… to play it again. I'm just not ready yet, okay?"

"Alright."

"I told Rory she could stay again since we are headed the same place in the morning," I said quickly before he could ask about her. "I hope that's okay."

"Oh, uh. Yeah." He nodded. He wasn't going to ask. He'd probably already forgotten she was there. "You two sure are spending a lot of time together. I know you're kind of into… I don't know. Did your mom and dad ever get around to having the talk—"

"Oh, no." I laughed. I knew where that was going. "No, she's just helping me with work stuff, you know. It's… it's not like that."

And it couldn't be.

"Gal pals, then."

I snorted. He had absolutely no clue what gal pals actually meant.

Chapter 13

The next morning, I was almost late. Nash was already gone by the time I'd gotten out of bed. I had to practically chug my coffee, and I was lucky my clothes were being tackled by someone else. I was rushing all over the place. I needed to be gone already. Shit, I was going to be late.

Then I bumped into Rory in the hallway.

"Oh, sorry." I laughed. "But good morning, Sleeping Beauty."

"You're in a hurry?" she asked, my joke having clearly gone over her head.

"Yeah, I'm late for work."

"Oh, right. Work." She forced a smile. "Stay away from the windows?"

There was a look of fear in her eyes. It had only been a few days. The idea of the weekend seemed lost on her. She wasn't ready to be alone again.

"You can come with me, if you want," I said without thinking.

Her eyes met mine.

"It's not like my boss could possibly hate me any *more*."

She nodded, fiddling with the bottom of my t-shirt.

"I think I have something for you to wear." I smiled, heading to my room.

If there were famous last words, "it's not like my boss can hate me more" would be mine. Because the look on my Madam Caron's face when I walked into the office, Rory in tow, told me she definitely could hate me more. I'd barely scratched the surface of just how much this woman could despise me, and just how narrow the slits in her eyes could get.

"*Marraine*," Rory whispered the moment Madam Caron came into view.

Rory's eyes lit up, and she practically rushed across the room to Madam Caron, her arms spread into a hug. I only just intercepted the awkward moment, which earned a handful of looks from the entire room.

"*Mon cheri*," Madam Caron called sarcastically, taking a rather large step back from Rory. "This is a place of business not... ah... social hour."

"She's here to help." I smiled.

"I have not extra work, finding something for you is difficult enough. I do not know who told you bringing friends to work was okay, but I'll be calling your uncle."

"Madam, please. She doesn't need any credits or letters of recommendation. She's just here to help me with my French. And there's no need to call Nash. He already approved it."

I could see Rory eyeing me out of the corner of my eye. She knew that he most definitely had not. But if I could keep my boss guessing, I was at least safe for today. Besides, it wasn't all that far-fetched given that Nash sprung my internship on her in a day. He was known for asking for forgiveness rather than permission.

"Ah," she sighed and grit her teeth. "But of course."

Madam Caron said nothing else as she made her way back to her usual spot at the center of the room. They ought to just paint a circle there so no one accidentally gets in her bubble or something.

"Why would you try to hug my boss?" I hissed the moment she was out of earshot.

"I... I thought I knew her." Rory looked down.

"I'm sorry," I breathed, trying to place the word she'd used. I couldn't.

She shook her head, but kept eyeing Madam Caron.

Rory followed me to my desk, where yet another list written in French sat atop my desk.

"I hate this place," I whispered as I picked it up. At the very least, my French was getting better.

Ironically, there was a reason Nash had chosen France as our first international branch. My grandmother, his and my father's mother, was a French-Canadian immigrant. While she'd passed when I was still pretty young, I'd heard enough of it spoken growing up that I should have known it much better than I did.

"Why do you do it if you hate it?" Rory asked as we sat down.

"I don't have a choice." I shrugged. "It's this or boarding school."

"Boarding school?"

"Yeah, it's… where parents send their kids away to live at school. So, I'd have to leave my home behind, and my friends. And…" I sighed again. "I'd be alone."

She nodded, but didn't say anything else.

I took a seat, pulling up my social media account before I even finished reading the list. No new messages from Molly. Good to know she cared. I thought maybe she'd come around. I closed the social media page. I guess I had work to do.

"I cannot believe people do this every day." Rory yawned as we were grabbing our stuff to head home. "I can barely speak."

"Thank you for all your help today." I smiled as we made our way toward the elevators. "Maybe they should have hired you instead."

She smiled back. "I doubt that. Even French is so different now."

She was clutching tightly to the blazer she'd borrowed that morning.

"Hey, it's okay," I said, touching her arm. "You'll get there."

She shrugged. "I am out of date like your computer. No one speaks Latin anymore."

"Wait, you speak *Latin?*"

She nodded.

"Rory, that's amazing! No wonder you're picking up modern English so well."

"But not modern French."

"You'll get it. We can even practice it together if you want."

"Really?"

I nodded as the elevator dinged. "What do you say we get some food and head home?"

She smiled and wordlessly followed me to where Henry was waiting for us.

"Girls." He nodded.

"Hello, Henry." I smiled.

Henry took us by a café where we grabbed dinner to go, and then straight home.

I went to my room and slipped into something more comfortable. Rory seemed to like being all dolled up, but I had a feeling this was dressed down from what she was used to. I didn't think it was smart to ask. The last thing I wanted after we'd had a decent day was to ruin it with my stupid mouth.

When I got back to the kitchen, Rory had our dinner all set out on plates. "You didn't have to do all that. I could have helped."

"I wanted to." She smiled.

Dinner was peaceful. Rory seemed to be much more comfortable while we sat with my French translation book, trying to make all our dinner conversations in French. It was good for me, but she was obviously much better at it than I was. In fact, she made a game out of learning new words quicker than I could. It would have felt unfair had it not been for the wide smile on her face.

"Okay, okay, you win." I laughed, closing the book. "My brain hurts."

"That is how I felt using the… computer." Her eyes were wide, like doing searches on the Internet had changed her outlook on life.

I got up and grabbed our long-empty plates and rinsed them off in the sink. "Well, you don't have to use it."

Behind me, Rory was cleaning the trash off the table, and by the time I'd finished with the plates, I had no clue what we were going to do with the rest of the evening. We probably still had at least another hour before Nash would even leave the office, and he was likely to grab his own dinner on the way home.

We'd only just settled down for a movie when Autumn walked in. She was on the phone, chatting it up, take-out food in one hand and Nash's dry-cleaning in the other. It was the most like his assistant I'd seen her look since we'd gotten off the McCoy plane.

When she saw us, she stopped short. "I'm going to have to call you back."

"Hi, Autumn." I smiled.

"Even...Rory. Long day today?"

I nodded. "Mostly because I'm not used to it."

She took the food into the kitchen and set it down, still clinging to the dry-cleaning.

"Even, do you think I could talk to you for a second?" She sighed as she turned around.

"Uh, yeah, sure." I nodded.

I followed her into the hallway, all the way to Nash's room. I lingered in the doorway while she hung up the dry-cleaning. I found it odd how well she knew the house. She adjusted her blazer as she came back toward me.

"I need you to be honest with me. Who is your friend?" she asked.

"She's an in—"

"Not an intern?"

I felt all the blood drain from my face. My throat got very dry.

"That's what I thought."

"Please don't tell Nash!" My eyes were already beginning to swell. "You know I can't get in trouble, and Rory—"

"Who is she?"

"I found her."

"You found her?" She raised an eyebrow.

"Yeah, she... she lost her parents... and I—"

Autumn sighed. She was buying it. It wasn't like it was a huge lie. I had found Rory.

"You're trying to help her?" Autumn asked.

I nodded.

"I'm not going to tell Nash—" she raised a hand up to stop me from thanking her. "But I think you should. He could help, you know he could. Especially if he knows the truth. And I don't think you should wait on it. Some of these custody situations take time, and you don't want to make things harder for her because of your own fear."

Chapter 14

The next day, Nash insisted we all get dinner after work. I wasn't sure if it was really Nash, or if it was Autumn. She had been spending more time with him lately, and from the moment he'd hired her, she'd been pushing him to spend less time at the office. I considered her on my side, at least on that front.

Even if she did want me to reveal the biggest secret of my life to him.

Regardless, Nash liked fancy things, so every time I'd been out to dinner with him, it was a dress-up affair. And let me tell you, if I'd been brave enough to wear jeans to a restaurant where his colleagues were wearing tuxes, it would be worse for him than underage drinking. At least my criminal record he could keep under wraps.

The moment we stepped out of the office, Henry took us back to the shopping mall. We spent the next hour there, because if Rory took forever picking out shoes, it should have been no surprise she took even longer picking out clothes. She loved getting to try them on rather than having them made.

Meanwhile, I literally settled on the first nicer-than-work outfit I could find.

"What do you think of this one?" I heard Rory's voice call, and I turned.

She was beaming in the doorway, giving a little twirl for probably the thirtieth time. I shouldn't have been awestruck, but I was. The dress was blue, a deep shade of blue that brought out her eyes. It fell just above the knee, showing enough thigh that they caught the eye. With a cinched waist and a chiffon fabric that draped over her chest, falling in a perfect sweetheart, I felt my cheeks grow hot.

"It's perfect." I smiled, looking down. I wish I had the ability to tell her to try on a different dress though. If she wore this one, I wouldn't be able to focus on dinner.

"Are you sure?"

I nodded, forcing myself to look back up. She was fiddling with the hem of her dress again.

"You look great," I insisted. "Now can we go? We're going to be late."

She sighed, rushed back into the fitting room to grab her clothes, and we were off to the register.

The restaurant was nearly across town. We were late, but when we walked in to join Nash and Autumn, Nash didn't seem angry. I assumed his calm had to do with the fact that Rory and I both dressed up, or maybe it was because Autumn was making him laugh. He laughed so rarely I'd forgotten what it even sounded like.

It sounded so much like my dad's it hurt.

116

"Are you okay?" Rory asked as we sat down.

I nodded.

"How was work, girls?" Nash asked, having not noticed my entire mood change, and it was Rory who answered.

"Good. Even's French is really improving."

"I'm hearing good things. Ev, how are you liking it at the office?"

"I wouldn't say it's my cup of tea." I shrugged. "But there are worse places to spend my summer."

"Oh, just tell her," Autumn said suddenly.

"What?" I asked, looking between them both.

"Okay, okay." Nash sighed. "You remember the planner for the summer gala? Elaine?"

I nodded. "Yeah, I did some work for her last week."

"Well, she's asked for you specifically to help her with the last-minute details."

"What? Me? But Madam Caron said—"

"Oh, never mind that." Nash shook his head. "Autumn was talking you up about the party you threw for me last year, and—"

"I just said you did most of the planning," Autumn corrected.

"Well, she was impressed with what you did, and she thinks you have a good eye for PR," Nash finished. "Which we will need at the gala. We have a lot of American-industry types coming this year, and she thinks maybe you can help her better connect with them."

"But I don't know anything about the American business industry." This was pressure. I didn't handle pressure. Planning a birthday party for Nash, one he didn't even show up for might I add, was one thing. Planning a major party like this, and we only had six weeks?

"Then you're lucky you aren't dealing with a lot of business people. You've been to our Christmas gala several times, it'll be fine."

Easy for him to say. It was hot in here, wasn't it?

Rory reached her hand over to mine, and I felt a lot of my anxiety melt away at the feel of her touch. I let out a breath and nodded to her, before I looked up to find Autumn watching us.

Autumn smiled at me, then went back to looking over Nash's shoulder at the menu. He was reading it for her. She apparently spoke just as much French as I had.

"Not sure if I'm even hungry anymore," I whispered to Rory as we opened our menus.

"You will do great," she said, squeezing my knee under the table.

"So," Autumn chimed in once we'd decided on our orders. "How did you two meet again? I don't think Nash has told me."

She was calling him Nash now, not Mr. McCoy like I'd always heard her do before. All his employees called him Mr. McCoy. The housekeeper, the drivers, the people at the office, and yes, even his beloved assistant. It was weird, but for some reason, it made me smile.

Then I picked up on what she was doing. She was trying to get me to tell him. Smart. Public setting, less chance of him making a scene. If nothing else, she knew my uncle better than anyone.

"Oh, Rory's an intern," Nash responded before I could even think about it.

Just then, the waiter came by, and I felt like I'd missed my chance. Next to me Rory had gone stiff as a board. She was so quiet, I wasn't sure she was even breathing.

"You okay?" I asked while Nash and Autumn were distracted by the waiter.

She shook her head slowly. "I'm scared."

"It'll be okay. I won't let anything bad happen, I promise."

I only hope I can keep that promise.

Chapter 15

I was going to tell Nash. I mean, I had to. It wasn't like I had a lot of options for Rory, anyway. There was no way I was brave enough to take her to another one of those shelters. She deserved better. I knew, even if it was deep down, I would have to tell him eventually.

I was going to do it the next day. Before work. He was always in the best mood first thing in the morning. After a long day, he was normally just tired and grumpy.

I woke up early, rehearsed what I was going to say, and waited until I heard him shuffling around. Then I took a deep breath and headed in to his room.

"Hey, Nash," I said a little too quickly. "I need to tell you… something."

He had a suitcase on his bed. His closet was open; his dry-cleaning, which Autumn had hung two days before, was hanging in his garment bag. His entire room was made up.

"Are you leaving?"

He let out a long sigh. "I'm afraid so. There's a situation back in Seattle I have to see to."

"Wh—what about me?" I breathed. It was barely over a whisper.

"Well, Henry will still be taking you to work, and Autumn will be checking in on things a bit more—"

"You're leaving me here alone?"

"I'll be back as quick as I can, Even." He sighed, reaching out to me. "It'll be just like all the other trips."

I jerked away. "The other trips you weren't leaving me in another country."

"I'm sorry. But you can't just quit the internship, and I can't ignore these issues, either. Autumn will still be here. So will Henry. You'll be fine."

I swallowed hard. "Yeah, fine."

I left while he was asking what I'd needed to tell him, ignoring the question completely. If he thought I was going to open up to him while he was abandoning me on the other side of the world, he was so wrong. And so was Autumn because I was sure she'd known he was leaving before our little heart-to-heart, too.

I wiped my cheek as quickly as I could when Rory walked in the kitchen. That was the last thing I needed her to see. I didn't want to explain it, either.

"Good morning, Sleeping Beauty." I grinned, trying to amuse myself.

"Why do you keep calling me that?" she huffed, crossing her arms. Someone wasn't a morning person.

"It's a movie about... well... you."

"Like on the TV?"

"Yeah, it's a cartoon—um, like a drawing, but it moves," I sputtered. How were you supposed to explain cartoons to someone who barely knew what a TV was?

"About me?" she asked.

"Yeah, sort of."

"I don't understand."

I let out a laugh. "We can watch it later if you want. We gotta get going though, or we are going to be late."

⁂

We stepped off the elevator and onto the third floor, and I felt like the looks I was getting were different somehow. Yesterday, I was shredding papers. Today, I was assisting with the planning of the gala? It was huge, but no one seemed jealous, which meant either they thought I deserved it (unlikely), or they didn't want to do it, and that was scary.

I let out a breath and headed over to the woman who'd talked to me the week before, when Madam Caron had insisted I wouldn't be of any help. I wondered if Nash had tried to get her to have me help then.

I was nervous. Nash had warned me about doing this, but that didn't mean I was really ready to jump into something like this. The gala was *huge* for McCoy Enterprises.

"My uncle told me you'd asked me to help?" I choked out as she looked up.

"Oh, *merci*," she called over the rather thick binder she was looking through. "I thought maybe you could look over what I have here and tell me what you think?"

"What I think? I'm just an intern. Don't—don't you have it mostly planned already?"

She nodded. "Yes, but… it has to be right. This is my first year here."

Of course, it was. "I'll give it a look."

She handed me a rather long slip of paper, handwritten in French. I was glad I had Rory. Looking back and forth between my book was hard, and I still wasn't great at this. There was hope that, with Rory by my side, I'd actually be able to get it done. From what I could read, I'd be incredibly busy that day, which was more than fine with me. Anything to keep on the good side of Madam Caron.

"And away we go," I whispered to Rory, pulling her toward my tiny desk.

She reached for the slip of paper and read it over carefully, frowning at some of the words. That wasn't a good sign.

"Do you know where to find all this?" she asked as we took a seat.

I shrugged. "More Internet searches."

She let out an exasperated huff. She hated the computer.

I actually knew a lot about the galas than I would ever admit to Rory or Madam Caron. Each branch of the company hosted their own charity gala each year. The French branch got the summer gala. Seattle went wild with a Christmas gala. New York typically did something for Halloween, and Chicago had a spring fling.

I'd attended Seattle's Christmas gala every year since I was eight. I'd only been to the New York one once, but I'd never attended in Chicago or France. I knew how things worked back in the states, but with the French branch being our first international location, I had next to no knowledge about how they did things. As much as our lovely party planner wanted my advice, I wanted to stay out of it completely.

All I really knew was that it was big. Everyone who was anyone attended, giving themselves a chance to dress up, wave around their money, and tell the press whose design they were wearing. I personally loved wearing off-the-rack gowns, because telling reporters the child of the McCoy's was wearing something from Sears just really tickled me pink.

I had a feeling I wouldn't be able to do that this year, especially not if I was able to bring Rory. I laughed to myself. Bring Rory. Like my date. Like that would ever happen. Who was I kidding? I turned my attention back to the task at hand. At least getting my work done was *possible.*

Luckily, the list was descriptive. Most of it just involved phone calls to confirm decisions Elaine had already made. None of what Elaine had done seemed like a bad idea to me. It was all pretty standard by way of party-planning.

She seemed to have thought of everything, too. Multiple meal options, allergens, parking, valet. There was no way I could have done all that on my own.

The rest of our job involved changing times of deliveries or addressing specific menu concerns. With Rory's help, her doing most of the talking., I was able to get that part done,

Picking up phones came rather easy to her, although she did seem to confuse people on occasion with some of the older terms she used. Slang had clearly changed a bit, and it wasn't like she spent most of her time around proficient French speakers who could correct her.

We finished the list by lunch, and I returned to an exhausted but grateful Elaine

"You have finished?" she asked, surprised.

I nodded. "All set."

"What did you think?" she asked.

"It all looked pretty standard to me. Look, if you're planning a beautiful party in France, the people who come expect it to be… well, French. I think you're worrying yourself too much."

She let out a relieved sigh. "I have more for you."

"Lay it on me."

And that was how I finally started doing well at work.

Chapter 16

Rory and I returned from work to an empty house. Nash was probably halfway back to Seattle by then. I was trying not to think about it. I wasn't alone. And it wasn't like I was used to Nash being around, anyway. Having him a 12-hour plane ride away was terrifying, though.

She had not forgotten about the movie. She asked about it the moment we walked through the front door. I was lucky Nash had so many streaming services, otherwise I might not have been able to find it.

I grabbed us some popcorn, and we curled up on the couch.

I was surprised at how close Rory sat to me. It would be so easy to yawn, stretch, and slip an arm over her shoulder, but I knew better. She'd likely scoot all the way to the other end of the sofa.

Or she wouldn't. Then what would I do?

As the movie started, Rory was mesmerized. She'd seen the TV for a bit the first day, but all we had was local channels and some basics on whatever plan the rental owners signed up for. We'd watched one movie, a few days before. And we had one TV that flashed news throughout the day at the office, but it wasn't a main focal point.

There was something special about watching a cartoon for the first time, seeing paintings come to life.

Then she gasped, "That is most definitely not how that happened."

Suddenly, she was sitting on the edge of her seat. "They would just send me off to the woods to live with fairies. That is absolutely something they would have done."

I chuckled, as her cheeks started growing more and more red.

"Oh, ew," she groaned as the on-screen Aurora began dancing in the woods with the prince. "Who is *he* supposed to be?"

"That's Prince Philip," I said, settling into the couch.

Out of nowhere, she threw some popcorn at the TV, hitting the Disney Philip in the forehead. I reminded myself not to mess with her—she had incredible aim.

"I would never dance with him." She scoffed. "He was an incorrigible ass who wanted *three* wives. Three!"

"Were you at least going to be the main one?" I grinned, stuffing handfuls of popcorn into my mouth. Rory was more entertaining than the movie.

She slapped my arm and went back to watching the movie.

"That is not how that happened, either." She huffed as the fairies brought the on-screen Aurora back to the castle and her loving parents greeted her. "Is this a joke? Tell me this is a joke."

"I didn't write the movie." I laughed.

"But you played it!" She hissed, only barely taking her attention off the screen. "I just go and prick my finger? Where did the spindle even come from?"

She was so heated about it her whole face having flushed as she raged about the historical inaccuracy of her own life. I found it absolutely adorable.

"Oh, no, Prince Philip will save her!" She rolled her eyes. I was pretty sure she'd learned that from me. "Yeah, let the dragon eat him!"

I nearly spit my drink.

"Ew, don't let him kiss me!" she said enraged, throwing more popcorn at the TV.

"You know, I'm going to have to clean that up." I grinned, and she picked up a handful and threw it at my head.

"What kind of happily ever after is this?" she fumed as the credits began to roll.

"The make-believe kind?" I shrugged, pulling popcorn from my hair.

"Is that really what people think of me?" She sighed, slumping back. It was the first time I'd seen her not sitting like there was a board on her back. "That I was some cursed child with loving parents who just wanted to save me from the evil witch?"

I shrugged, swallowing hard like her question had just taken all of the humor from the room. In a way, it had.

"Most people…" I sighed. "Most people don't think you were real at all. They think you were just a story made up for children."

"Clearly I am not."

"Clearly," I agreed, feeling her hand brush against mine. I wanted to hold it. Why did I want to hold it? "So how did it happen?"

"Even." She pulled her hand away, fiddling with the blanket between us for a second. "I'm tired."

She stood and went back to her room, and I felt myself slump in my seat. Every time we started to have a moment, she pulled away. Or I did, I suppose. It was me who did the leaving in the alleyway.

⌾⌾⌾

I was just ready to head to bed when I decided to check in on Rory. She hadn't left her room once since the movie. I tapped on her door, and heard a sniffle in response. I opened it.

"Hey," I said, leaning against the door frame.

She was sitting on the ledge of the large window, looking out at the city. There were streaks of tears down her face and the remnants of old ones dotting her shirt. No, my shirt. She was wearing my pajamas again.

I didn't ask, though I should have, but crossed the room anyway. I opened my arms and let her curl up in them.

A big part of me wanted to ask her about it. What made her so afraid? What had her crying by herself in her room? Was

129

there anything I could do to help? But I didn't. I just held her. I knew asking made her pull away, and I just wanted to be there for her, even if I didn't know why she was hurting.

"Thank you," she sniffled after a few minutes. "I'm sorry."

"It's okay." I nodded. "Listen, if you don't want to talk about something, just tell me. I won't press, okay?"

She nodded, wiping her face with her hands.

"But," I sucked in a shallow breath, "I'm here if you do want to talk."

She nodded again, swallowing loudly before reaching out and hugging me again. I felt a chuckle escape my lips. Rory fit perfectly under my chin, in my arms. And with her touch came a feeling I didn't think I should be allowed to feel for her—home.

"HELP!" I called, feeling panic swell within me. I started sobbing, but kept calling. No one came. No one could get me out of the car.

But I wasn't in the car. I was in the tower—that tiny room Valerie's stupid friends had locked me in. But, both doors were locked. I couldn't get out. I couldn't breathe. I was going to die.

"Even?" I heard a soft velvet whisper call into the night, and I sat up.

"Yeah," I breathed, struggling to calm down, center myself, get out of that headspace.

"Are you okay?"

"Yeah, yeah. I'm fine. Just a dream. Did I wake you?"

"No," Rory sighed, standing sheepishly in doorway. "I couldn't sleep. Do you think I could—"

"Yeah, come in." I rubbed my eyes as she came around and crawled into the bed next to me. "Any reason why you can't sleep?"

"Dreams, I think," she said flatly, but there was something about the dismissive nature of her tone. It told me she knew what she was talking about.

Maybe she remembered more about the curse than she was letting on. We honestly hadn't talked much about it. We'd barely talked about her old life at all. I was too busy trying to catch her up on what she'd missed, trying to help her blend in. I didn't think about it. In a way, that made me much too similar to Nash for my liking.

"You can talk to me about it." I sighed, lying back down next to her. My bed was cold now, probably covered in sweat, but I wasn't about to complain.

"It's nothing."

"You sure?"

She nodded, and even in the dim glow from the street lights outside, I could see the slight glisten that had grown in the corners of her eyes. "I just don't want to be alone."

Her voice broke, and suddenly she was crying again. I pulled her into my arms and let her cry. Sometimes you needed that—to just cry.

"I'm here," I whispered into her hair. "You're not alone."

We stayed like that for a while, legs tangled together, our breath falling in sync until she slowly stopped crying. But she didn't pull away. She just stayed in my arms. Somehow, we must have drifted off to sleep.

When I woke the next morning, Rory was still curled into my arms, clinging to my midsection. Her hair was practically in my mouth, but I didn't dare move. It was the most at home I'd felt since my parents were alive, and I held onto those moments before she woke up like they were oxygen.

The house was still. I was glad Nash wasn't here. I really didn't want to explain this to him, especially not after insisting we were just friends. I also didn't want to explain to him why I was so drawn to her. I couldn't even really explain it to myself.

I had woken Sleeping Beauty, that much was clear. But what did that really mean? Was I her true love? Were we destined to be? If that were the case, which it wasn't, why was she so afraid of me when we'd first met?

I let out a sigh, to which Rory responded, "Good morning."

She didn't move, which made me wonder how long she'd been awake. That was perhaps even more confusing.

"Good morning," I said back, looking down at her. "Have you been awake long?"

She shook her head softly. "Only just."

Still she didn't move. In fact, her grip on my midsection just might have gotten tighter, which was both intoxicating and comforting, especially since I could feel her fingers gently trailing my spine. Why was she doing that? And why were her feet still tangled with mine? And why was she just letting me run my fingers through her hair? Why was *I* doing that?

"Even?" she asked, her voice barely over a whisper.

"Yeah?"

"What was your dream about?"

I felt myself stiffen. No one had ever thought to ask me before. Which meant I'd never had to say it out loud. The memory of my parent's death haunted me nightly for the last three years. I'd never had to tell anyone the exact details of the worst day of my life. Or how those details had changed the very fiber of my being so much that I didn't even know myself.

She pulled away enough to look up at me, her blue eyes expectant as they looked into mine. I took a deep breath.

"I lost my parents a few years ago." I swallowed, and she tucked her head back under my chin. "It was an accident, but it was really bad...um." I sighed. "They died, and I have dreams about that night a lot now."

She didn't say anything for a moment. She just kept running the tips of her fingers up and down my spine.

"Did you love them?" she asked finally.

"Very much."

"Were they nice?"

"They were the—" I choked for a second. "They were the best people on the planet."

She nodded, tucking her head under my chin again.

"What was your family like?" I asked after a moment.

It was her turn to stiffen, and stiffen she did. Her entire body went rigid, and her fingers stopped moving against my back. I was glad I couldn't see her face.

"I barely knew them," she said flatly, lacking any emotion, which told me rather quickly she was most definitely lying.

"Oh."

She sighed, and we were both quiet for a moment before she spoke again.

"They were cold and cruel," she said finally, "And I didn't know them. Not really. It was my… godmother who raised me."

"I'm sorry. I'm sure you miss her."

She nodded dismissively and pulled away. Clearly, she was finished with that conversation.

Rory didn't come back out of her room until it was time to leave for work. She skipped the small breakfast I'd made, and I was already headed to the car when she caught up. We rode all the way to the company in silence, which even Henry seemed to pick up on.

I didn't know how to make this better. Or keep from messing up. Or get close to her because the truth was, it had been a long time since I'd wanted to get close to anyone. I kept Molly at an arm's length for multiple reasons, but the biggest one was that I couldn't afford to lose anyone else.

Chapter 17

Elaine set us to work organizing a seating chart over the next few days, which wasn't finished by the time she handed us a catalog of decorations to order.

I was in charge of décor. Just me. She gave me no guidance, only the theme, and told me to "run with it." I had artistic freedom. What did she even mean?

It had Nash and Autumn written all over it. "Oh, Even is artistic. She's super creative, she's so great at decorating. Did you see the photos from this party she planned this one time?"

Nash was always down to give me projects I didn't ask for. Like the painting he had me do for the office. I hated that thing.

Yes, I'm creative. Yes, I'm artistic. Yes, I picked out decorations for one party this one time. But that was a birthday party. Not a summer gala, which brought in thousands of dollars for charity and even more in revenue from the friendly negotiation that went on during the gathering.

Maybe I didn't know everything about the stupid company, but I new damn well Nash made deals on gala nights. All of them did. Post Christmas, Seattle was always booming in business. New year, new networking, or however the saying goes.

"Are you alright, Even?" Rory asked.

I'd begun angrily flipping through the pages. All this stuff was so cheap, plastic, and disposable. I thought Nash was big on green and recyclable. I sighed.

"Yes," I huffed. "No, there's no way we can use any of this stuff."

I stood up and went to find Elaine. I had to evade Madam Caron to get there, which was becoming less of an issue, as she normally got distracted by Rory.

Elaine was hunched over the seating chart Rory and I hadn't gotten to finish, arranging a new set of labels we hadn't even had.

"What did you find?" she asked cheerily.

"I really don't think we should use any of this stuff." I sighed, and she looked like a might have slapped her. "What I mean is... McCoy Enterprises started the green initiative last year, so it wouldn't be right to have a bunch of disposable decorations. Do you think there's a theatre in town that would let us borrow props? Or maybe we could use the general décor of the venue to our advantage?"

"We're in the venue." She sighed. "I don't know what the Seattle branch budget is, Even, but ours isn't that grand, I'm afraid."

I nodded. "Think you could show me the plan, then?"

After Elaine and I finished tossing ideas around while standing in the largest conference room I'd ever seen, it was nearly time to head home. I hadn't seen Rory since Madam Caron had started chatting her up. We really hadn't talked much that day.

It was reassuring to find her beaming at me when she met me in the lobby.

"Ready to go?" she asked, handing me my jacket.

"Yeah." I nodded. "Thank you."

"Did you and Elaine figure out the decorations?"

"I think so. It'll be a process to actually figure out where we are getting them, but it'll look good in the end. What about you? How was your day?"

"I learned to use the copy machine." She grinned like kids do when they've learned some cool new trick.

"Oh yeah?" I laughed.

"Yeah, I jammed it."

When we got home, Rory and I sat down for dinner. I was becoming too used to this. I was too used to her presence. I was too used to the way she talked and laughed, the sound of her voice, just the feel of her near me. I'd been alone for a long time. Having Rory around felt so peaceful, it was foreboding.

"Are you alright, Even?" Rory asked as I was cleaning the dishes.

"Yeah, I'm just... tired." I swallowed hard. I hated lying.

"Maybe you should rest."

She reached up, brushing the hair from my face in that same soft, tender way she'd done before. Her hand met mine on the counter. She was inched closer. Her hand hadn't left the side of my face.

"Maybe." I swallowed hard.

Dammit, why was this girl so intoxicating?

The sound of the key turning in the lock had the two of us apart so quickly it was sickening. Autumn walked in the door, Henry in tow, with armfuls of grocery bags each. Both Rory and I had to scurry out of the way in the tiny kitchen.

She looked between me and Rory with this judgy look. She knew I hadn't told Nash about Rory. She knew I'd just let him leave town unaware. Maybe I should have told him. He could have simmered on the plane. But I was angry, and I knew it was childish, but I didn't care.

"Even," Autumn sighed as Henry headed back out the door. "Could I talk with you for a moment?"

Without a word, Rory slipped out of the room, leaving me alone with Autumn.

"You realize you're playing a dangerous game, right?" Autumn sighed. "Do you even know where she came from? Do you know she didn't lie to you about—"

"Yeah, I do." I groaned. *But I can't tell you the truth, so…*

She sighed, calming herself. She was so much like my mother sometimes. Maybe her and Nash would work out after all.

"Even, you've got to tell Nash."

"Nash isn't even here, Autumn! He left me in another country."

"He has work to do."

I clinched my jaw. I was going to say bad words.

"He's trying to do what's best for you. You should be a little more appreciative. Don't you understand he's trying to help you? And protect you—"

"He's avoiding me, like he's always avoided me. He puts the company over me, and I'm an after-thought. I have to get in trouble for him to even sleep at home. If I don't get arrested, I don't see him for *weeks*, Autumn! You see him every day. I see him six times a year if I behave. And I'm supposed to be *appreciative* that he left me in another country?"

"Even, you need to be careful—"

"No, fuck you, Autumn." Oops, I said bad words. "You don't get to tell me I should be more appreciative. You don't get to tell me what to do at all, actually. You aren't my mom, okay? Nash is my guardian. He should be here. He should be the one who noticed I lied. He's the one who should be talking to my teachers and checking up on me. Nash is the one who should be talking to my therapist. Not you. I'm pretty sure it's basically a violation of HIPAA or something."

"Are you done?" She raised an eyebrow. I didn't answer. "If you don't tell Nash about Rory, I will."

"Tell Nash about Rory, go ahead," I growled, crossing my arms like a child, but I didn't give a damn. "You think it'll help things? Because it won't, and I'll never trust you again. You know as well as I do, Nash hates the messenger when it comes to bad news. And I know for damn sure you're trying to keep yourself on his *extra* good side."

"What the hell is that supposed to mean?"

"Don't think I don't see the way you look at him. Don't think I haven't noticed how you're calling him Nash instead of Mr. McCoy. I see you Autumn, I freaking see you."

"Whatever you think is going on between me and your uncle is strictly between me and your uncle," she huffed. "We are adults. We make our own decisions."

I scoffed. I couldn't argue with that. She was going to just rub this "ten months from eighteen" shit in my face.

"Like it or not, Nash is still responsible for you," she said, calm again. "And if you want what's best for her? You need to tell him the truth, Even. Sooner rather than later."

She grabbed her purse off the counter. "Some of those groceries are cold. You might want to put them away." Then she stormed out, slamming the door shut behind her.

Before I could even stop myself, there were tears streaming down my face followed by deep, painful sobs. I wanted to curl on the floor.

Rory rushed into the room, and her arms were around me so quickly I couldn't think to tell her no. I couldn't wipe my face and pretend I was fine. I'd just have to settle for letting her see the ugly side of me.

I couldn't decide if that was okay.

Rory had been in bed for a while. After I'd stopped crying, I'd asked for some space. I needed it. To think, to breathe, to just… be. I was about to put away my sketchbook when I accidentally kicked my guitar. I grabbed the strings as quickly as I could, but it was still loud as hell.

I waited. I didn't hear anything, so I started putting things away, then I heard a knock at the door.

Rory poked her head in. "Are you okay?"

"Yeah." I laughed. "I just bumped my guitar. Sorry, I didn't mean to wake you."

"You didn't. I cannot sleep."

I sighed, biting my lip. "You want to talk about it?"

She shook her head, rocking on her heels.

"You can stay in here if you want." I smiled, gathering up the rest of my things off my bed. "All you had to do was ask."

Her cheeks flushed a bright red, but she didn't say anything. Instead, she helped me with my stuff and climbed into the bed. I flipped off the bedside lamp, and flopped down. She curled into my arms and let out a long sigh.

"Better?" I asked.

She nodded. "How are you feeling?"

"I'm okay... I think."

"She was hard."

I felt myself frown. "Harsh?"

"Yes." She giggled.

"She was right about some things, though." I sighed. "I do need to tell Nash about you... I'm just not sure what to tell him at this point."

"And you cannot tell him the truth?"

"The truth? That I woke up a 15th century princess?"

Rory laughed. "I suppose not. Do you think he will help me?"

There was pleading in her voice, along with a hint of fear.

"Yeah, I really do." I let out a shaky breath. "As much as I hate to admit it sometimes, Nash is actually a pretty good guy."

"And you will help me, too?"

"Of course, I will."

"Do you believe in true love?" she asked all of a sudden.

"I—" I let out a breath. "I didn't used to, but yeah, I guess. What about you?"

"I have to believe it. Without it… without it I would not be here with you."

Her grip on my waist got tighter, and she tangled her legs with mine. A soft sigh escaped her lips as she put her head on my chest, just under my chin.

She fell asleep rather quickly after that. I stayed awake, listening to her breathe. It was calming… soothing.

I was thinking about what she'd said about true love. A part of me hoped I could be. I shouldn't have been letting myself feel that way. I was getting attached, and I knew it was dangerous.

Then her breathing got a little quicker. Her body started twitching, mostly her hands, and she started mumbling. It was just incomprehensible at first. And then she said "*non*" once or twice.

No, and *please.*

I was going to let her sleep, wait the dream out. Sometimes waking from the dream before letting it end was worse. I knew that all too well.

But once she started crying in her sleep, I knew something was wrong.

"*Pere.*" she said. The word for father. "*Pere*, please."

"Hey," I whispered, "Rory, wake up. It's just a dream."

She took a deep breath and blinked up at me.

"Catherine," she whispered, and before I could stop her, she pulled my face to hers, pressing her lips to mine.

I breathed in, feeling my heart begin to pound. I was torn as my body told me one thing and my brain another. My initial reaction was to pull her closer, because even though I knew it was wrong, it felt right. Her lips moved against mine in a way that was strikingly familiar. It wasn't technically our first kiss, but somehow, this felt like it could have been our thousandth.

I pulled away, partly because she was dazed enough to think she was kissing someone else, and I knew it was wrong to take advantage of that. But I also pulled away because kissing her made me feel things I absolutely could not feel.

She looked up at me, her face caressed by the moonlight, or maybe it was streetlights. I couldn't be sure. Her eyes went from that knowing gaze to the same frown she'd developed in the tower. She was out of the bed before I could move.

"Rory, wait," I whispered, grabbing onto her wrist before she could reach the door. "Please?"

I took a shaky breath. I knew better than to stand, my legs would probably give out. Whoever Catherine was, Rory had loved her more deeply than I'd loved anyone in my entire life. I didn't know if I was capable of love like that. I didn't think she could take being broken-hearted twice. But, something about her made me want to try.

She didn't say anything, but she didn't pull away, either.

"Who was Catherine?" I asked. I knew it was probably the wrong question. The only question I could ask to make her pull away and shut me out. I couldn't stop myself from asking anyway.

"You look like her," she whispered, looking back at me for a second. There were tears falling down her face again.

I stood and pulled her into my arms.

"You even feel like her," she spoke into my shoulder. Then she was sobbing.

"But I'm not her…" I swallowed hard. *I'm not her, and I never will be.*

So much for fairytales and true love.

"No." She shook her head, looking up. "But you're here."

I nodded, and she kissed me again, sending a wave of energy coursing through my body. It wasn't gentle or soft; it was passionate—hungry. Maybe I shouldn't have, hell I *knew* I shouldn't have, but I kissed her back. I took in as much of her as I could while it lasted.

Suddenly, she was inching our bodies back toward the bed, and I felt my heart begin to pound furiously against my eardrums. Her hands were on my waist, my bare waist, as I stumbled against the bed, sitting down. She didn't let a single inch make its way between us as she climbed on top of me.

I could feel our breath growing heavier. My hands found her waist just as her hands started sliding down. A quick breath escaped my lips, and I pulled away.

"Wait," I breathed, grabbing her hand that had just barely slipped beneath the elastic of my pajama shorts.

I let out another shaky breath.

"What's wrong?" she asked, tucking her hair behind her ears.

"I, um." I breathed. Fuck, it was hot in here. "I just… I don't know if now is the best time—"

"Even?" *Shit, please don't say my name like that.* "Are you okay?"

I nodded. "I just… um." Why was my breath so shaky?

She reached up and pushed a strand of hair out of my face. It was so soft and tender. I didn't think anyone but my mom had ever been that gentle with me. The touch pulled my focus back to her. "It's okay."

I bit my lip. How did she end up being more experienced than me?

"You've never done this before, have you?" She asked.

I shook my head.

She nodded slowly. "It can wait."

She kissed me again, but it was different. It was soft and sweet, and when she pulled away, she pressed her forehead to mine. It was the most intimate I'd ever been with someone, and something told me it was unlikely I'd ever feel something quite like this again.

Chapter 18

Of all the things I thought I, an English-speaking high-schooler, with a poor ability to understand French, would do while in France, seeing a movie was not one of them. Just like movies in the US are in English, movies in France are in French.

They aren't slowed down or dumbed down for English-speaking people. There are no captions in English for me to read. They aren't made easy for any reason. Why would they be?

But while watching TV earlier in the week, Rory had seen a preview for a movie that was out in the theater, and how could I tell her no?

So, we got tickets, grabbed some snacks, and sat as far to the back as we could get on a Friday night. Before sitting down, I hadn't thought about how awkward this would be. We hadn't really discussed the kiss, or what had almost followed, and we hadn't really touched again since.

As the lights grew dim, and the movie began, I found my hand inching toward hers. I knew better. She'd only kissed me because of the dream. The dream about Catherine. Not the dream about me. I wasn't what she wanted. Yet a part of me, the part that just ached to be shattered to pieces, hoped I could be.

My hand inched closer and closer until my fingertips brushed hers, and I just left it there, waiting for her to respond. I knew what no response would mean. If she didn't respond, it was likely she didn't want to hold my hand, and therefore wasn't interested in me as me. Which was fine, I could handle rejection, but I'd rather get it out of the way now before I grew more attached to her.

She gave me far too much hope though, lacing her fingers in mine without a second thought. I felt my heartrate soar. I knew I was done for when she leaned her head against my shoulder. Yep. I was screwed.

It was worse because we stayed that way the rest of the movie. Her hand in mine, her head on my shoulder, her other hand wrapped all the way around my upper arm like it was a pillow. I hadn't been on many dates, so it wasn't like I had much to base it on, but this definitely felt like a date.

Especially when on screen, French or no French, these two were in love. Or lust. I couldn't be sure. There was a lot of kissing and other things going on, but I couldn't really understand everything else in the plot. I just knew they'd gone from strangers to something much more.

People didn't see movies like that with just anyone, right?

The credits finally rolled after a rather dramatic happily ever after that put a knot in my throat. I'd never have anything like that. I'd never get to call someone mine forever. Everything is temporary.

"You ready to go?" I asked, struggling to look down at Rory, as people around us began filing out.

She shook her head slightly, still clinging to my upper arm. But she didn't say anything, so I just waited. I wasn't sure what I was waiting for, but if she needed me to wait, then I would.

The crowd had all but disappeared when she let out a long sigh and let go of my arm, sitting up. She held onto my hand, though, which I had to admit fit far too perfectly in mine for reason. I stood, pulling us up the aisle toward the exit.

"Even, wait," Rory breathed, grabbing my upper arm and pulling me to a stop. I was glad there was no one behind us.

"Yeah?" I turned; she was fidgeting with the hem of her shirt again. That nervous tick of hers.

"I am not ready to leave because...er..." She sighed, looking up at me for a moment, then back down at our entwined hands.

"Because?"

She swallowed audibly before looking back up at me again. No, not at me. At my lips, distinctively at my lips. There was a brief pause before her eyes drifted up to mine.

I could have been wrong. I could totally have been seeing things. If that were the case, she had every right to stop me, or slap me, or whatever she saw fit. But I took that brief glance at my lips as an invitation.

Her hand slipped from mine as I took a step toward her and slipped one hand around her waist, and the other at the nape of her neck. A gasp slipped from her lips, and I paused just long enough for her to pull away, say no, shove me off. But she didn't.

So, I kissed her, pulling her closer to me until there was no space between us. I heard a soft moan as she kissed me back. Her hands wrapped around my waist, and I felt them lock together. For one short moment, the world was ours, spinning into eternity. I didn't care about where we were or where we had to be.

Until I heard a male voice echoing toward us in French. Cue record scratch. We pulled away, both of us turning toward the sound of the voice. The lights had come back on, and he was in to clean up. Last showing of the night, it looked like from the sheer number of lights overhead.

Rory giggled softly, covering her mouth, and took my hand. We headed toward the exit, Rory offering a soft apology over her shoulder before we were both laughing again. I couldn't decide if the look on his face was because of the time, the fact that we'd just lingered in the theater, or that we were both girls, and I didn't quite care.

We were halfway to the car, where Henry had likely dozed off, when I pulled her back to me. She was still grinning, and when I looked down at her, her face grew suddenly serious. I pulled her to me and kissed her again. This time, it was the clearing of a throat that pulled us apart.

The clearing of Henry's throat.

I looked up to find him standing by the open rear door. My throat was dry. Shit. Shit, shit, shit. If Nash found out about this... ugh, if Nash found out about *me*. I swallowed hard, struggling to find my voice.

"Henry, I—"

"It's getting late, Even." He smiled softly. No edge. No tension. He didn't seem to mind the lateness for himself, but rather, he had a protective stance he seemed to develop whenever he took us places where he couldn't follow and play bodyguard.

I nodded, letting go of Rory's hand as we rushed over toward the car.

"Please don't tell Nash about this," I whispered to him just after Rory had climbed in.

"I'm not sure it's my place to." He nodded, gently ushering for me to climb in.

I did, sliding all the way over to where Rory was seated. I offered her a smile, which she returned, blushing as she did so. Her hand reached for mine, and I took it, feeling far more comfortable doing so than I should have. This wasn't built to last, and I knew it.

Chapter 19

I started to live for the nights when Rory needed me, the ones where she'd find me before I went to bed, or when she slipped into my room in the night. She quieted my dreams. There was a rather specific comfort about her that kept all of my pain at bay, and it was terrifying.

I hated depending on other people. When you depend on people, it's easy to be hurt when they're gone. Depending on others means the moment they leave, there's a hole where they should be, and I had enough holes as it was.

I didn't say so, though, and I never turned her away. Despite knowing it would get me hurt, despite knowing I'd grow unreasonably attached, it was ridiculously hard to say no to something that just felt right.

"Even, are you awake?" Her velvet voice called into the night.

I was now. "Mhmmm."

"No, you are not."

She rolled over, facing away from me.

"Yes, I am." I sighed, pulling her closer to me. "Are you okay?"

She nodded wordlessly.

"Why are you awake, then?" I was awake now. I wasn't sure what time it was, but until I was sure she was actually okay, there was no going back to sleep.

"The dreams again." She rolled back over in my arms.

"You want to talk about it?"

She stiffened. I thought she might pull away, rush from the room, shut me out. Maybe it was because I was holding her, I didn't know. She sighed instead.

"No, I..." She reached up and touched my face so softly it gave me goosebumps. "I only wanted this."

Her lips met mine, and then I was really awake.

I felt my stomach get all fluttery as her hands wrapped around my face, pulling me in with no protest from me. I was careful to place my arms on her waist as she continued to caress my tongue with her own. She inched her way on top of me, and I was struggling with any logical means of stopping her.

My heart was racing like it did any time she kissed me, especially as those kisses made their way across my jawline and down my neck to my collarbone. My breath became ragged as her hands brushed against my bare skin. She was making it harder and harder to say no, but I just wasn't ready.

She didn't seem to mind just doing this, whatever this was. This kissing, cuddling, touching around the clothing thing she did when there was something serious she didn't want to talk about. It was a distraction. I knew that. And I fell for it every time.

Maybe I needed it, too. The distraction, the touch, the feeling of being wanted and needed. I knew even then it wouldn't last forever. I knew it was temporary, but so were all the other highs I chased so religiously.

Chapter 20

Nash had been gone three and a half weeks. I didn't care to text him. He hadn't really checked up with me. He was having Autumn do it, and Henry saw me every day, too. Both of them would report back, so I had resolved to not tell them anything I didn't have to.

I didn't know when Nash would be back, or why he was gone so long, but I was determined to keep my word. Stay out of trouble, do well at the internship, and even though falling in love with Rory wasn't really on the agenda, I guess I was determined to do that, too.

One day, things began to change.

"Even," Elaine said as she reached my tiny desk. "I have an important vendor meeting that has been rescheduled today, do you think you could take over for me at the committee meeting?"

"Take over for you…" I breathed. "As in run it? As in, I'd be in charge?"

"Yes, I know it's short notice, but—"

"I'm just an intern."

"And you're the best intern. You're the only person I trust to know what they're doing on this. Please?"

"Yeah, I got it." I forced a smile, only reassured when Rory put her hand on mine as Elaine was walking away.

"You'll do great." Rory smiled.

The crazy part is I did do great. I'd only met a couple members in the committee, mostly because as much as they were called a "committee," they were really just a bunch of McCoy executives who had to approve all of Elaine's financial and design decisions and concur as a group the choices were right.

No one seemed surprised to see me. I wasn't exactly the face of McCoy Enterprises, but anyone who worked there knew my face and my name. I didn't even have to speak French during the meeting, and nothing was vetoed.

In fact, they loved our take on following the green initiative.

At some point after that, I stopped being an intern. I mean, technically, I was still an intern, but Elaine stopped asking me to do things, and started having me make the decisions. I'd missed how it happened, but it felt like the roles were reversed. I was calling the shots. And somehow, it wasn't as nerve-wracking as it should have been.

Rory was still helping with all the plans. She was with me every day, at least when she wasn't off chatting with Madam Caron.

I didn't have any experience planning a gala, but Rory did. It was a little crazy how much her opinion had begun influencing my decisions.

"I just love parties." Rory sighed, as we walked through an aisle of fabric table cloths we were trying to choose from. There were too many, plain and simple.

"Oh yeah? Did you have a lot of them?"

"Not a lot, but..." She paused, eyeing a white silk cloth pressed with flower designs. "When we did, they were grand like this."

I bit my lip, thinking through what I wanted to say carefully. I didn't want to ask the wrong thing or make the wrong comment. This was the most she had talked about her life before the tower.

"Did you have a fancy party planner like Elaine bringing them to life?" I asked finally.

"No, it was my job." She smiled.

"What? Really?"

She nodded. "One of the few things I was allowed. One of the few things that brought me joy, even though Airard was always there, always my dancing partner."

"How long had you been..." I sucked in a breath. "Nevermind."

"Betrothed? Since birth."

A silence set over us. I didn't have a good response to that.

"I really hated him," she said finally. "I hated who he was. I hated the idea of him. I was never going to even like him, much less love him."

"And I'm guessing you didn't have much of a choice." I sighed.

She shook her head for a moment before her eyes lit up and she dashed off, grabbing a sage green table cloth in front of us.

"This is the one." She grinned.

Chapter 21

The gala was one month away, and while I was happy with my notion to wear an off-the-rack gown from whatever department store was available in this part of the world, Rory was apparently not. After seeing the designer gowns several of the other girls were flaunting around the office, including Madam Caron, Rory had her heart set on something similar. I hated parties like this, but as it turned out, they were kind of her thing. Big shocker there.

So, despite all the teeth-pulling, I followed Rory into a relatively small boutique Autumn had suggested. It wasn't custom designer; with only three weeks, there was no time for custom anything. But it was definitely still designer.

There was lace and tulle in every direction, and in far more colors than I ever could have imagined fabric could come in. Gowns of so many sizes, shapes, and cuts. Mirrors lined the back near a narrow set of fitting rooms. Rory was in heaven, and this was my nightmare.

Rory went first, mostly because she was picky, but also because I thought it would be nice for us to match. Finding something that went with whatever she picked would be much easier, more so because I genuinely didn't care what my dress looked like. But if my past shopping experiences with her told me anything, it was that we'd be here all day. Literally.

Still, the smile on her face made it worth it. Even as she tried on probably the fiftieth dress. It turns out every color is her color. Me, personally? I like her in blue. Stupid fairy can keep her pink.

"What about this one?" she asked, doing the best turn she could muster in the mermaid style dress she'd donned.

"I think if you can barely turn or walk, you're going to have trouble dancing." I grinned. "But other than that, it looks great."

She let out an exaggerated sigh. "Why don't you pick something, then?"

Someone's getting hangry. I didn't say that. Instead, I got up and started eyeing the racks while she slipped back into the dressing room. It took me less than two minutes to find the perfect dress. I handed it to one of the associates before sitting back down.

Rory and the girl started muttering to each other in French after a moment. With the hushed tone, I could only pick out so many words, but if I was honest, I wasn't paying much attention. Not until Rory poked out her head.

"Pick something for yourself." She smiled.

That would be a trick. By some miracle, the only color they didn't have was black, which was odd because everyone in this city wore black on a daily basis. The closest I could find was grey.

I sighed, eyeing the dress like it was my enemy. Girly and dainty with lace and frills. There was nothing wrong with the two on principle, but neither described me. But it would match the one I picked for Rory, so I handed it to one of the other girls and awkwardly headed toward one of the other fitting rooms.

As I stepped in, the girl followed to assist me with the dress. I sucked in a shallow breath. This was one of the biggest reasons I didn't get fitted for dresses or go into these stupid shops. Getting undressed in front of anyone was physically painful. Having someone see my scars was the worst feeling.

I mostly kept my back to her. Even with the mirror, it made me feel better. The girl didn't comment. In fact, I didn't even see her look at my scars, which was a relief. Instead, she focused on getting the gown in all its thin lacey glory off the hanger.

Just as I'd gotten undressed, I heard Rory gasping from outside the room. Sneaky brat waited until I was in here to check herself out in the mirror. I should have seen that coming. The girl who was helping me only got me halfway in the dress before Rory was already back in the fitting room next to me.

I eyed myself in the mirror in the dressing room for a moment. It looked great from a physical standpoint. Made my reasonably sized boobs pop, my waist look thinner than it actually was, and by some miracle, the pieces of lace on the sleeves covered my burn scars.

"Would you like to see the larger mirror?" I turned in the dressing room, eyeing the back of the dress as best I could.

I shook my head. "This is it."

The girl looked surprised.

I sucked in a breath as I started to look at the tag, and then dropped it again. I didn't want to know. Nash said dress to impress for this one. I didn't need to know. Just get the stupid dress.

"Even?" I heard Rory call. "Are you alright?"

"Yeah," I called back, turning to the girl. "Can I take it off now?"

She nodded hesitantly and helped me get the dress back off, turning to leave while I put my regular clothes on. She still didn't seem to notice my scars. Either that or she was just very good at being polite. A+ customer service.

"Did you find one?" Rory asked. She was back in the knee length floral print dress she'd donned that morning.

I nodded. "You?"

She rolled her eyes. She was getting too good at that. "Yes, the one you found was *parfait.*"

"Will this be all together?" one of the girls asked as she hung the dresses back up into garment bags.

I nodded, grabbing the card Autumn had given me that morning. Henry met us outside, and took the garment bags.

"I'm going to take a wild guess." I sighed as we climbed into the car. "You're hungry?"

She laughed. "Yes, actually."

Chapter 22

Three weeks left to the gala. Nash was still MIA, with promises he would definitely be back in time for the gala. Autumn was on my case about telling him about Rory. Elaine and I were stressed over finalizing everything, but for the most part, things had gone off with few hiccups. Maybe it was the McCoy funds talking, I didn't know.

I was still doing everything I could to get Rory adjusted to the real world. When I wasn't spending time kissing her, that is. I had mostly forgotten how limited my time in France was. Between the time I put into planning the gala, and all the time I was spending with Rory, I was too distracted.

The summer was nearly over, and apparently all I'd really done was fall deeper and deeper for her. I just hadn't really admitted it to myself yet.

Everything was perfect. We had the house to ourselves, we had Henry taking us basically wherever we wanted, and we had each other. It felt like nothing could ruin how perfect life was. For the first time in a long time, I was just enjoying life.

⚬⚬⚬

Much to my surprise, renting a couple bikes was not only cheap, but easy. Teaching Rory how to ride one would be a different story altogether. All the ways this could go horribly, horribly wrong were already running through my head, but she was beaming as I returned with them, and I couldn't change my mind then.

I hadn't ridden a bike in years. Not since before the accident, when I rode a bike to school instead of a well-secured SUV.

To be safe, I'd gotten both of us helmets, Henry had found knee and elbow pads, and I'd made her wear a pair of my jeans, which were too long, but would hopefully provide some sort of protection. I would have wrapped her in bubble wrap if I thought she could still pedal, but that was unlikely.

We went to a large park where she could learn to ride on something softer than concrete. I found us a spot far from other people, trees, or playground equipment and parked our bikes. Henry was around here somewhere. Nash had him watching us a lot more closely these days.

"Okay." I sighed, biting my lip as I had Rory climb on. "It's pretty simple. You just pedal, like this to go, squeeze this to stop."

She nodded, giving both of the break bars a squeeze. I'd have gotten her training wheels if they'd been available, but they weren't.

"But don't just squeeze the front, it's not fun." I grinned.

"Even, I don't think this is a good idea," She mumbled. "I changed my mind."

"You can do this. It's easy. I'll hold you up for balance. All you have to do is pedal."

"You won't let go?"

"I won't let go," I lied.

She got off to a great start, pedaling pretty well, keeping her own balance. She'd eventually fall. After the first two times I let go, she was pretty much done trusting me to hold her up, but she wasn't ready to give up riding the bike just yet. Especially not when I hopped on and rode it like it wasn't a big deal.

We had been at the park nearly four hours when she finally figured out how to ride the bike, by which point we were both exhausted. I flopped down on the grass and handed her a bottle of water.

It was a beautiful day—gorgeous, really. Blue skies, fluffy clouds, the perfect temperature. Even with Henry lurking around somewhere, albeit out of sight, I couldn't have imagined a better day.

That is, until the police showed up, and we left the park in handcuffs.

Chapter 23

There wasn't time to run. There wasn't even time to react. We had no warning. I didn't hear sirens or see any lights. They barely even said anything when they approached us.

When they did speak, they were rattling off so quickly in French I couldn't keep up. As we were being walked back to their cars, I caught sight of two lovely gentlemen I recognized. The two from the halfway house I'd taken Rory to. Freaking jerks.

Rory was crying, asking me what to do, but I couldn't answer. I was going numb. My brain was racing as I went through a spiral of all the things that followed.

If Henry could see us, he would call Nash. If not, I'd have to call him from the police station. He'd be furious. They wouldn't let Autumn pick us up because she's not my parent, like always. Nash would have to fly back.

I was dead meat.

They put us in separate cars, which was absolute agony. The only solace I had was that the one I was in was behind the one they'd put her in. I could see her head bobbing in the back window.

She didn't deserve this. Being arrested for the first time was terrifying, and it was all my fault she was in this mess.

They booked us, took the mug shots, and took us down separate halls, nowhere near each other. The last time I saw her was when they got our fingerprints.

I was brought into a room where they asked about the halfway house. They asked why we ran. They asked about Rory. God, they had so many questions about Rory. They concluded I was American and a minor, and promptly ended the conversation, at which point I was walked to a cell.

Nearly an hour later, I was allowed to make a phone call. I should have called Nash. I knew he was who I should have called, but Nash wasn't there. He was in Seattle.

I called Autumn.

"Even?" she nearly shrieked into the phone. "Why are you calling me? You should be explaining yourself to Nash!"

"Yeah, well." I sighed. "Nash isn't here, so… I'm guessing he already knows?"

"Henry called him as soon as they took you. And then he called me to try and figure out what happened. Even, what the hell were you doing?"

"Nothing! We were just… we were just riding bikes in the park."

"People don't get arrested for riding bikes, Even." She mumbled something I couldn't hear.

"Okay, okay... I tried to find a place for her myself," I grumbled. "Before you found out. Before anyone knew about her. It was some... I don't some halfway house or something."

"You took her to a halfway house?"

"I know. I know it sounds bad, but she was desperate, and so was I. Once I realized we were in trouble we got right out of there—"

The phone beeped twice.

"Shit, I think I'm out of time on this thing. Listen, just tell Nash... tell him I tried to do the right thing, okay?"

"Sure, Ev, I'll—"

The line went dead. I let out a long sigh before hanging it up and getting walked back to the cell I'd be waiting in for the next eleven or twelve hours.

This was different than the system they had in Seattle. I wasn't waiting in the lobby. I was waiting in an actual cell. They hadn't even told me what my actual offense was, but I was pretty sure they'd tell Nash. I didn't know what Rory was arrested for, either.

I just hoped we weren't *arrested,* arrested. I hoped they were holding us like they did in Seattle. A part of me knew that wasn't the case. There was a good chance Nash couldn't get me out of this. Getting in trouble in another country? Not my brightest move.

The jingle of the cell door woke me. I was walked out, down a few halls, and into a lobby where Nash was waiting with Autumn.

He was furious. Beet red, sweat on his forehead, hands-in-fists kind of furious. He didn't try to hug me. He didn't smile at me. He wasn't happy, which I knew full well I deserved.

But I didn't care about that. What I cared about was the guard had locked the door behind me. And Rory wasn't here.

"Where's Rory?" I asked.

"Probably still in holding." Nash sighed, exasperated. Long flight? "I don't care, let's go."

I didn't move, crossing my arms. "I'm not leaving without her."

"Even, I get that you've gotten close, but someone else can come get her—"

"She doesn't have anyone else!" I yelled. "And I'm not going to just abandon her in a jail cell."

"You are trying my patience." Nash gritted his teeth. "I said, let's go."

"Excuse me, sir?" I said to the officer behind the counter. "If he paid any bail, go ahead and refund it. I'd like to be rebooked."

Nash was at my side fast, pushing me away from the counter. "Don't be ridicu—"

"No, Nash, you don't be ridiculous." I smacked his hand off my shoulder. "I am not leaving without her. So, you can do whatever magic you have to. I'll go to jail in Seattle, I'll go to boarding school. I don't care. Just get her out."

"Why do you think for any reason I should be doing you favors right now?"

"It's not for me, it's for *her.*"

"Don't pretend like you aren't getting benefits out of this," he sneered.

I could have slapped him. Instead I eyed Autumn.

"Oh, no. This isn't about me," he snapped. "This is about you. You and your lies, your deceit, and your *obsession* with trouble."

"I don't have an obsession with trouble," I groaned.

"You seem to cause a lot of it. And you've got no self-preservation. Did you really walk across a city in another country by *yourself* just to keep a secret?"

"Yeah, I did." I let out a breath. "I don't know why, I just... did."

"You don't know why you do anything you do," he scoffed.

Autumn reached out a hand brushed across the back of both his shoulders.

"No, actually, I do know," I snapped. "I was scared. Do you have any idea how fucking *lonely* it is up in that penthouse every night by myself? You told me I'd be going to *jail* if I got in trouble here, or boarding school. So, you can bet your ass I was willing to do what I had to. Because I knew you'd already given up on me, anyway. You didn't want to listen."

"Even..." He sighed.

"You know," I scoffed, "I went through something incredibly traumatic at a vital age, and rather than getting me therapy, rather than just being *around* when I needed you, rather than listening to a damn word I said, you expected me to just be fine. I'm not fine. I haven't been fine for quite some time. But you're never there to see that. Yeah, I do stupid things. Because getting high is the only thing that keeps me from reliving it, and getting in trouble is the only thing that makes you notice. But god dammit, Nash I didn't do this on purpose, and Rory didn't do anything wrong. Please. Get her out."

"Nash," Autumn sighed. "Do it."

Chapter 24

I don't know what magic Nash had to work. He was on the phone for a good minute before he even talked to the officer behind the counter. The officer was on the phone for what felt like forever. But finally, finally, Rory was walked out of the same door I was.

She was crying when I wrapped her up in my arms. She mumbled something to me, but I couldn't really understand her. I tried to shush her, calm her down enough to get a comprehensible word out. By which point, Nash was really done, and he basically shoved us out the doors.

We rode back to the house in separate cars. Nash and Autumn in one, me and Rory in another. I had a feeling that was for the best. Being in close quarters with Nash probably wasn't the best idea.

"Even, go to your room, pack your things," Nash snapped as we stepped into the house. "You're going back to Seattle. Whatever this is," he pointed between me and Rory, "It's over."

A knot rose up in my throat. I pushed Rory behind me. No way was I letting her get in the middle of all this.

"No, Even, don't do that," Autumn said before I could even turn away. Nash reared on her, basically seething. "Go to your room. Nash and I need to talk."

"Autumn, it's really not your place—"

"So, help me, Ignatious McCoy, I will walk out of this door and out of your life."

Nash swallowed hard. No one used his full name. There was a lot of power behind it. He stormed off to his room.

I waited until they were all the way there until I followed. Rory was poking her head out the spare room door, her lip trembling, while I stood eavesdropping.

"I thought you said spending summer in juvy was an empty threat!" Autumn hissed, barely above a whisper. "Is that really what you think will solve this? Did you not listen to a word she said at the police station?"

"It was an empty threat, Autumn, until it wasn't." He let out a sigh, and I heard him flop down on the bed. "I don't know what to do with her. She's clearly incapable of staying out of trouble, no matter what she says, and I can't trust a word that comes out of her mouth."

"She didn't do this on purpose, Nash, but I think you know that. She was trying to do the right thing, and I think she did pretty well for being left by herself in a foreign country."

"She wasn't by herself. She had—"

"She didn't have *you,*" Autumn groaned. "Don't you get it? She doesn't need me and Henry. She needs you. You're the only family she has left."

"Autumn..." He sounded defeated.

"I know you're trying to protect her—"

Protect me from what?

"—but I don't think this was the way to do it. And I know you're mad. She lied to you, but I think... I think if she hadn't had Rory, she'd have done a lot worse. She's worked hard. She's not even smoking anymore."

"You knew about Rory," Nash said. It wasn't a question. And he was pissed.

"Yeah, I figured it out," Autumn sighed.

"You *figured it out?*"

"Yeah, Nash, I figured it out."

"How? Why didn't you tell me?" he snapped.

"Because she needed to tell you." Autumn sighed. "And because I paid attention, something you don't seem to do when it comes to Even. You expect her to be just fine, well, she's not."

"I don't know what I'm doing." His voice cracked. It actually cracked. I could have sworn I could hear him crying.

I peered around the corner to find my normally gruff, collected uncle sobbing into Autumn's stomach, clinging to her for dear life.

"I didn't want this," he choked out.

Of course, he didn't. He didn't want me. He never did.

173

"I didn't want to run the company," he continued, "And I'm not built for parenting. I failed her."

"You didn't fail her," Autumn whispered. "But if you send her away instead of showing her you'll always be there for her, you will."

I turned back to Rory, who was still watching me tentatively. I grabbed her cheeks in my hands and kissed her before I slipped back to my room.

I really didn't want to get caught.

A knock came at my door a few minutes later. Nash poked his head in to find me pulling things out of my closet. I had a feeling I wasn't going back to Seattle, but I had half a mind to run away, anyway.

I looked up at him, but kept ripping things off hangers.

"Ev, why don't you sit down?" He sighed.

"Did you come in here to yell at me?" I swallowed hard.

He shook his head.

"Okay."

He came over and sat down, rubbing his face with both hands. I pretended not to notice.

"I need you to tell me what you can about Rory," he said finally.

"Are you going to help her?" I bit my lip, feeling my eyes swell.

"I'm going to try."

I let out a sigh. "What do you want to know?"

"How did you meet her? That's a good start. The real story this time."

"I found her," I said carefully, "By herself, in the... woods."

"The woods? Even, what the hell were you doing in the woods?"

"You got a house parked up against a nature reserve. I just... I just took a walk."

"And she was just alone out there?" he asked.

"I mean, so was I?"

He took a deep breath and let out a sigh. "So, then what?"

"She was scared, and I offered to help her." I sighed. "And I tried, that's why I took her to that place."

"Even, why didn't you just tell me? You know I have friends here. You know I have connections. We could have gotten her settled from the beginning."

"I was just scared, I guess."

"So you just went off on an adventure to a halfway house."

"Yeah," I sighed. "I didn't know it would go like that. And we only ran because... because you said if I got into any trouble... And then how could I help her?"

"Are you sure she is who she says she is?" he asked.

"I'm positive."

"Alright." He nodded, letting out a long sigh as he stared at a blank point in the wall. "I'll make some calls. She... she can just stay here in the meantime—"

"Thank—"

"I wasn't done," he continued. "I don't think you should be bringing her to the office anymore. Or the gala. That's a disaster waiting to happen, especially if we find out she's—"

"She's what? A criminal or something?" I let out a laugh. "Nash, what do you think I am?"

"Even..."

"She's been an amazing help at work." I bit my lip. "She's the only reason I've done so well. And she deserves to be a part of all this just as much as anyone else."

"When is Autumn not right?" He let out a soft laugh.

"What—what do you mean?"

"You and Rory... there is something going on, isn't there?"

I swallowed, opening my mouth to answer, but it took too long.

"Yeah, I thought so, too." He sighed. "You're not going to just let her go, are you?"

I looked down at my hands, biting down hard on my lip to keep my eyes from swelling.

"I can if it's what's best for her."

"That's probably the most grown-up thing I've ever heard you say." He grinned.

"Yeah, don't get used to it." I gave his shoulder a shove.

"I owe you an apology," he sighed after a minute.

"Nash, can we not, I'm tired, and I—"

"Let me get this out."

I nodded for him to continue.

"You were right earlier." He cleared his throat. He hated admitting he was wrong about anything. "I should have been there for you. I shouldn't have thrown myself into work. I should have thrown myself into taking care of you. I didn't know about the dreams... I—and that's not an excuse. I would have known if I'd been there."

"Nash..." I sighed. "You never wanted kids; I get it."

"Nah, that's not it." He scrunched his nose. "I can't have 'em. Not possible. But being handed one that's mostly grown... I thought I'd do best by you if I didn't try to be your dad. I'm never going to amount to what he was. I know that."

I let out a soft chuckle.

"I'm sorry, Ev. I should have been there. But, I'm here now. I—I'm trying."

I nodded, feeling my eyes start to swell.

"And when we get back to Seattle, I'm going to be around more, I promise."

I looked up, and a single tear escaped. "Okay."

He leaned over and gave me a one-armed hug. That was more like the Nash I knew. Then he wasn't all over again.

"I love you," he whispered into my hair before he stood and left the room without another word.

Three words I hadn't heard once since my parents died. They clung in the air like a thick fog. Suddenly I was sobbing. It was one thing to know you were loved, feeling it implied, but hearing it is something else entirely.

Chapter 25

I'd thought Rory would be out of there in no time, headed off to some foster home to adjust to real life. Nash had a way with working magic. I always thought it was the money.

A part of me was okay with that. I knew it was what was best for her. I was only in France for the summer, anyway. I'd let myself grow far too attached. But another part of me was blissfully grateful there was nowhere else for her to go.

My and Nash's rooms weren't far apart, and Nash had never been known to talk quietly.

"…she's sixteen years old," he was saying as I slipped out of my room and stood outside his door in the hall. "Because she told me, that's how I know."

There was a long pause. Nash was getting tense. I could see his back grow rigid as I peered over the doorframe.

"She's lost them… No, I don't know how!… Yes, Aurora King, that's what she told me… Yes, I'm sure she's French, why would I say she was if she wasn't?... She told me... why would she lie about that?..."

My heart was pounding. It wasn't like anyone could possibly guess the truth, I knew that, but what would they do otherwise? It wasn't like we had any ID for a girl who'd been born in the 15th century.

"I'm positive she's not an illegal immigrant..." He scoffed. "No, she doesn't have any identification on her... You're sure? And what do we do with her in the meantime? Yes, I can manage just fine, but that isn't the point... Yes, I have a niece her age... Yes... For how long? I'll see what I can do. Thank you, Paul."

He got up. I darted back to my room as quick as I could, trying desperately not to make any noise. He was going to give me the short version anyway, but that didn't matter. Nash didn't like it when I eavesdropped.

I lunged for my bed the moment I made it into my room, and reached for the first thing I could find. My sketchbook, but it wasn't even open by the time Nash stepped in. So much for acting natural.

"Oh, good," Nash sighed as he stepped in. "You're awake."

"What's up?" I asked, tossing my sketchbook to the side like I'd actually had it open.

"It looks like Rory will be staying with us for a while. My lawyer has been in touch with the officer in charge of her file and..." He sighed. "It looks like they're having trouble finding any record of her in the system. So for now they're treating her like an immigrant, and the placement system takes some time."

I was a little shocked. That wasn't the short version, even though he'd left out the part where they thought she was an *illegal* immigrant. I had a feeling neither of us felt like taking on that subject.

"Okay." I shrugged, trying to be nonchalant.

"I think she'll be a lot happier here with us than in a shelter, so…" He let out another tired sigh. "I guess you can talk to her?"

"Yeah." I nodded.

He nodded back and tapped my doorframe before stepping back out.

I'd only just stood when Rory stepped into my room.

"Heard all that, did you?" I asked.

She nodded.

"Are you…okay with that?"

She hadn't said much on the subject. I think she'd hoped we'd never be a part. I wanted that. I did. It just terrified me.

"Do I have a choice?" She shrugged; gosh, I was rubbing off on her way too much. "I thought that… maybe…"

"I want you to stay." I felt a hitch in my breath. "But I also want what's best for you."

"And you think that it is not you?"

I nodded, looking down. I couldn't look at her.

"You don't…" She let out a shaky breath.

I looked up. Her bottom lip was quivering in that way it did when she was anxious. She also had the hem of the pajamas I'd bought her in her hands, twisting it.

"I don't what?" I asked.

"Nothing," she said, quickly darting from the room.

I tried to follow her, but I heard the lock of her door latch before I could even get out of the room. What the hell had I done now?

Chapter 26

I was back in the woods, and I was running. My feet weren't moving as quickly as I knew they should I could run faster than this. Why couldn't I run faster than this?

My heart was racing. There was somewhere I needed to be, and fast.

The wind was howling, I could hear twigs snapping off in the distance, and other footsteps echoing all around me.

"Even?" I heard Rory's voice echo, followed by a shrill scream.

My feet wouldn't go faster. I couldn't get to where she was. I couldn't—

"Even?" I heard Rory's voice, and I was instantly awake. "Are you okay?"

I sucked in a shaky breath. I was sweaty again.

"Yeah," I whispered back. "Yeah, I'm fine. Just a—"

"Bad dreams?"

I rubbed my eyes. "Yeah."

"Me too," She said meekly, shutting the door behind her.

"I'm sorry—" we both said at the same time.

"Come here?" I asked, holding my arms out wide.

She didn't hesitate. Her legs curled up with mine and she let out a soft sigh the moment her cheek touched my chest.

"Better?" I laughed.

She nodded.

I let out a sigh.

"What are you thinking about?" she asked.

"Life, I guess. The future."

"What about it?"

"I don't know." I let out a laugh. "I guess I don't know what I want to do with my life."

She craned her neck to look at me in the dim light. "You don't?"

I shook my head. "I really have no clue. Something creative, maybe. What about you? What do you want to do now that you don't have a kingdom to run?"

"I like working at McCoy Enterprises, actually."

"What?" I giggled. "No way."

"Yeah, I like the people, and I feel like… I feel like I'm helping."

"Well, I mean, if that's what you want to do, I guess you're lucky you know the owner's niece, huh?"

She shrugged.

"What do you think you want to do there?"

"I think I'll be an intern." She sighed.

I tried not to laugh. She was being so serious.

"Oh, honey." A sigh escaped my lips. "People become interns because they want to do something else."

"Like what?"

"Well, Elaine was an intern once, now she's the head of Public Relations in Lyon."

She let out a huff and aggressively tucked her head back under my chin. "I don't know what I want to do, either."

"That's okay, you have time to figure it out."

I started running my fingers through her hair, and she was asleep soon after.

Chapter 27

Rory was ecstatic, having learned that not only would the gala be a big party, but it would also be a *ball*. Once Elaine mentioned the dance floor, Rory couldn't stop talking. She didn't often talk about her old life, which I'd grown accustomed to, though I wished I could have earned her trust enough.

But balls, those were something she went on and on about the entire ride home. She talked about how big they'd been, calling people from every kingdom nearby. The fashion was a topic that lasted nearly half the drive home, and she was still on the dancing when Henry pulled up in front of the house and gave me a playful nod.

She was still talking about one ball in particular she remembered from right before she went to sleep as we walked up to the house.

"You have to make sure there's traditional dancing. Something beautiful, *non?*" She smiled as I set down my stuff and headed to the kitchen for a snack.

"I'm sure people will dance." I shrugged as I made my way back to the couch with a handful of grapes and sat down. I watched as she twirled around in the baby blue knee-length chiffon dress she'd donned that morning. She wasn't much for the monochromatic ensembles a lot of French people were into these days.

"You too, I would hope. You cannot plan it and sit out all night."

"Oh, I don't dance."

Rory stopped, her shoulders slumped over ever-so-slightly and she turned to me with a look of pure horror on her face.

"You don't?" she asked.

I shook my head, a playful smile toying at the corners of my lips. She was so shocked by this, and the puzzled expression that fell across her face was absolutely adorable.

Nash walked in the front door just then, looking from Rory to me.

"Everything okay?" he asked.

"*Non*, it is not!" Rory groaned. "Even does not dance."

Nash let out a chuckle and shrugged. "They don't let you dance in cuffs."

Was that a joke? I threw a grape at him as he made his way to the kitchen.

"What? It's true!"

"This is not funny!" Rory continued, "How can we have a ball if we do not dance?"

"I'm sure everyone will dance but Even." Nash smirked, poking his head back in. "She tends to hide in the corner at these things, anyway."

"I do not!" I did. I shrugged. "I don't even know how to dance."

"I will not allow it," Rory huffed softly, putting her hands on her hips. "Will you dance with me?"

I groaned as I considered it. While I would love nothing more than to have Rory so close in my arms, twirling her around like I had in my dreams, the idea of actually dancing, tripping, falling, making a fool of myself, kept flashing through my mind. I puzzled too long. She threw her hands in the air.

Nash stepped back in, munching on a bowl of cereal. "Come on, Ev. It's just like riding a bike. It'll all come back to you."

"Dance with me," Rory pleaded, coming over and sitting on the couch. She took her hands in mine and made this pouty face she'd been working on all week, pretty much since we'd watched *Avatar*. "Please?"

It worked perfectly. How do you say no to that face? That adorable puppy dog face, and those big blue eyes, and those pushed-out lips that are just inches from your own.

"Okay," I sighed forcing a smile. "Teach me the ways of the Force."

She frowned.

"I've got to find a copy of *Star Wars*."

Rory dragged me to my feet and into the center of the living room. Much to her luck, and my dismay, there was plenty of room.

"So, what do I do?" I sighed.

"Your hand goes here," she said matter-of-factly, setting my left hand on her hip.

Then, right in front of Nash, we were pressed together, our faces only inches apart. I looked up, but Nash was on his phone. I felt my throat dry out, my breath shaking as I looked back down at her. My hands were sweating already, and we weren't even moving yet.

She started stepping from side to side. I was pretty sure we were supposed to join our other hands, until she reached her left hand under my right and started raising it, then let it fall. Once, twice, three times.

Rory slipped from my arms, turning one way, then the other, returning my hand to her hip as she forced me to shimmy around the room like I should have known what I was doing. She did the hand thing again, this time with my left, forcing my right hand onto her hip.

She turned again, around me, with me, around me again. When she finally slipped her hip back into my left hand, she also slipped her hand into my right one, where I'd originally thought it should be. Then we were turning, doing some two or three-step shimmy thing. It looked great when she did it, but I could hardly keep up. Every time I tried looking at my feet, she'd lift my chin again.

She finally did a few turns under my arm before she stumbled into my arms, or maybe my arms stumbled into her. I couldn't be completely sure. But our labored breaths mingled together for a moment before a laugh escaped our lips.

"Nobody dances like that," I whispered.

"*Non?*" She smiled. "You just did."

I felt my cheeks grow even hotter.

"Did you study dance, Rory?" Nash asked, popping his head around the corner.

We practically jumped apart, and Rory nodded to him.

"It was part of my studies." She smiled, looking between the two of us.

I was sure she'd only looked at me to confirm she'd not said the wrong thing. I shrugged.

"That was beautiful. Maybe we could find your old teacher."

Nash ducked back into the kitchen. It felt like Rory and I both let out a breath at the same time.

"You want to go do some more planning?" I swallowed. "For the gala."

Rory nodded, her eyes never leaving mine.

I grabbed my stuff from the couch, waving to Nash as we headed to my room. Once we were in and the door was shut, Rory was in my arms, her lips on mine, her hands in my hair.

She pulled away. "Please say you'll dance with me at the ball."

"Gala." I smiled, biting my bottom lip.

She rolled her eyes and tilted her head at me.

"Okay, I will dance with you at the gala."

She grinned, stretching up to kiss me again, just as I heard Nash's footsteps in the hall, and tossed her toward the bed while reaching toward the closet.

"Hey, Ev." he said, poking in his head. "Any dinner plans?"

I shrugged. "No?"

"Great, Autumn's picking something up."

"Autumn, huh?" I smiled.

"What?" he asked.

"Nothing, not a thing. She's just been spending a lot more time around lately. The whole summer, really."

"Well, she's my assistant, so—"

"Uh-huh."

He cleared his throat and slipped back out of the room, closing the door behind him.

Chapter 28

One week until the gala, and things were falling into place, orders were arriving, and everything was confirmed. This was the time for catastrophes. This was the time when everything went to shit, it all fell apart, and everyone started to panic.

But that didn't happen.

There was no major mix-up with the linens, there wasn't a shortage of some rare menu item, and all of the auction donations arrived on time. We weren't rushing about fixing this or that. We were on schedule.

How was that possible?

I chalked it up to Elaine's impeccable organization skills and Rory's help with literally everything I did. Elaine told me things were running smoothly because of me—I knew better. I couldn't have done all this alone.

What I hated, though, was that I despised McCoy Enterprises less and less each day. It wasn't just that I got to spend all day with Rory. Planning the gala was fun, even if I wasn't looking forward to actually attending it. In fact, the only part of the gala I was really excited about was seeing Rory in her dress.

The dresses had been delivered the Wednesday before the gala, which cut things rather close, but you couldn't rush perfection, I suppose.

⁂

The day before the gala was my last official day of the internship. We would only be in France for three days the next week. Nash insisted we would need that time to pack and get settled. I wasn't sure what that meant.

Elaine and I did one last run-down of our checklist to confirm times, people, orders, catering, and the seating chart. Most of it was exactly as it had been, everything seemed in order, and nothing seemed out of the ordinary, so she sent Rory and I home early, before it was even time for lunch.

I was really going to miss her.

With all the work we were doing on the gala, I'd had little time for fun. I think that was the point of the internship, and maybe even why Nash had insisted I help with the gala. The gala had taken over most of my life, and I felt like I barely had time to spend with Rory, even when she was curled up next to me every night.

When Henry got back to the house, Rory went off to change, and I went for another cup of coffee. From the kitchen window, I could see the pool glistening in the hot sun. It called to me like ice cream after a long day and coffee in the morning. Here we had a pool, a large pool with a deep end and everything, and I'd yet to use it once all summer. At the very least, I had the rest of the day.

I set down my cup with a grunt and headed off to my room to change. Rory knocked just as I slipped on my one-piece suit, poking her head in.

"Where are you going?" she asked.

"Swimming. You want to come? I have another suit."

"Okay." I reached back into the closet and grabbed the two-piece I'd most likely never put on.

"I'll meet you in the living room." I smiled while she eyed the suit curiously.

It was a good minute before I heard her coming down the hall. It's not like she had a lot of experience putting on bikinis. When she stepped into the living room a few moments later, I found it hard to look at her, but even harder not to. She looked dangerously good in a bikini. Whoever said princesses were picture perfect was absolutely right.

"First things first," I choked out before clearing my throat, "we both need sunscreen. Between your porcelain skin and my pasty nonsense, we'll both be lobsters by lunch."

"Lobsters?" She frowned.

I shook my head, a laugh slipping out my lips. "Just turn around."

I sucked in a shallow breath. Any time I touched her; it was intoxicating. Her skin was smooth and soft, and just looking at it made me want to kiss her all over. And here I was about to smear sunscreen all over it. There was so much exposed skin. Like, an entire back of exposed skin.

I'm a weak sack of shit.

"You okay, Even?" she asked, looking over her shoulder.

193

"Mhmm." I nodded, forcing myself to squeeze the sunscreen onto my hand.

I let out a deep breath, and just went for it.

Listen, I know putting on sunscreen isn't supposed to be an intimate thing. But when the person you're putting sunscreen on can make your stomach tie in knots just by existing, it takes simple tasks to a whole new level.

She turned as I finished with her back, and wordlessly took the bottle from my hand before squeezing some of it into her own.

"Your turn," she whispered.

My knees nearly gave out, but I swallowed hard and turned around, grabbing my hair, and pulling it out of the way. I still hadn't removed the cover I was wearing. Was I shaking? I was shaking. Rory had never seen my scars before.

"Even?" she whispered after a moment.

I let out a breath and took off the cover. And then I waited. I waited for the gasp that usually came any time someone saw my naked legs, feet, and back. I waited for the tuts, or the questions. But they never came. She just smeared the sunscreen on my back like there wasn't a stretch of bubbled, scarred skin from my hip nearly to my shoulder.

"All done," she said softly.

When I turned, she was smiling like nothing was wrong. Nothing had changed. Nothing about my back made her feel awkward or queasy. Which made me feel more accepted than I ever had.

We finished putting on sunscreen. Rory laughed loudly as I dabbed it on her face, leaving huge globs on her nose, which basically started an all-out sunscreen fight until we both had far too much of it on our faces and in our hair. But we were giggling and happy. So, I left the cover on the floor as we headed out to the pool.

I ran and did a flip into the deep end. Doing flips into a pool was possibly the most acrobatic I'd ever been. Maybe if I'd learned a little parkour, I'd be better at getting away from the cops. But as Rory smiled when she joined me outside, something told me I might not be doing that anymore. Getting in trouble now meant I'd be running from her.

"Come on," I called, treading in the water. "The water is the perfect temperature."

"I might just say out here." She shrugged, hugging the towel I'd given her.

"You don't know how to swim, do you?"

She looked down and shook her head.

I inched my way to the shallow end of the pool.

"Do you trust me?" I grinned.

"Even, it's—"

"Do you trust me?"

She nodded.

"Jump in."

"But I can't—"

"Just do it." I laughed. "Trust me. I've got you."

Her eyes met mine for a second, contemplating, then she dropped the towel and jumped in, a tiny squeal escaping her lips as she splashed next to me. She sank for a second, touching the bottom before she stood up all on her own. She hit me on the shoulder.

"Why didn't you tell me you could touch the bottom?" She rubbed her eyes and glared at me.

"Where would the fun have been in that?" I laughed. "Besides, I said you could trust me, didn't I?"

She leaned in and kissed me, the taste of chlorine mixing with the taste of her. I was glad Nash was still at work, because I absolutely did not want to have to pull away.

We spent most of the day in the pool. I taught Rory the stupid games I'd learned as a kid. Between those and small make-out sessions, we stayed distracted enough that we managed to reapply sunscreen about two times less than we should have. Laughing and smiling with her made me feel like laughing and smiling was a good thing again, not just something I did when I felt sarcastic.

She followed me inside for lunch, both of us dripping on the floor a tad from the front door to the kitchen. I pulled out stuff for sandwiches, and she wrapped her arms around my waist from behind.

As I pieced together our lunch, she planted kisses all over my back, right where my scars were. It made it hard to focus on the task at hand, but no one had ever done anything like that before. No one had ever made me feel like my scars weren't something to gawk or laugh at.

When I turned around, her expectant blue eyes stared up at me. I inched toward her, slowly, my face just inches from hers. Then I took a huge bite of my sandwich and took off toward the patio, Rory in tow.

When evening descended, we traded our damp towels for one of the blankets from inside. The house sat just far enough from the nature reserve to see sunset from the pool deck, and we sat there, in silence, waiting as the dark took over the city. The stars began poking through the darkness, tiny twinkles of hope.

"It looks different," Rory whispered after a few moments.

"What does?" I asked, still staring up at the sky.

It was weird being able to see the stars again. I was so used to a constant cover of clouds and rain, and I'd forgotten there could be so many. Tiny twinkling diamonds shining back at me. They were all so beautiful. It made me miss the meteor showers my parents had taken me to see as a kid.

"The stars. I remember more of them."

I nodded, pulling her closer. We were curled up together on a single pool chair, wrapped in the blanket for warmth. The temperature had dropped tremendously, and I was regretting having not changed out of this swim suit, but no way was I getting up when she was so close to me.

"If I'm honest," I sighed, "It's been a long time since I've seen so many. I hear there are some amazing places to see stars in Seattle, but..." I scoffed. "My friends are lame."

Rory took a deep breath and let it out.

"What's Seattle like?"

"Oh," I sucked in a breath. "It's um... rainy, mostly. Busy, lots of traffic. Everyone's always drinking coffee with somewhere to be. And there's graffiti everywhere. But when the weather clears, it's really beautiful. There's a lot of art, and there's some amazing food."

Rory nodded. "You like it?"

I shrugged. "It's home."

Saying the words put a sour taste in my mouth. Seattle wasn't really home to me. Sure, I lived there, and I had found some amazing things about it, but Portland was home. Portland was where I'd always hoped to return. Even so, sitting with Rory in my arms, Lyon was feeling more and more like home every day.

"Well don't you look cozy," I heard Nash laugh from the gate. "You girls hungry?"

Rory nodded, rising from the chair before I could even think of a response.

Chapter 29

The irony of the gala was increasingly humorous to me. A Renaissance ball, which Rory had grown incredibly excited about. When the night finally came, I was, too.

Nash had arranged for our hair and makeup to be done at a local salon, along with Autumn's. I think he wanted us to bond, but she didn't say much, and she was rushing out before they'd even finished the complicated updo they'd decided on for Rory. She had to get back to her hotel and get dressed before Nash came calling.

We, however, got dressed at the house like any normal day. I felt absolutely ridiculous wearing such a big bulky dress as I looked in the mirror. I looked like a princess. I scoffed at myself. Princess of mischief, maybe.

"Even, the car is here," Nash called to me. Why was he waiting on us? He still had to pick up Autumn.

"Coming," I called back.

Rory was still in her room.

"Rory, everything okay?" I asked through the door.

"Yes, I'm almost finished," she called through the door. It was labored, but I wasn't about to press. If she needed help, she was more than capable of asking for it.

"Well, don't you look stunning." Nash smiled as I stepped into the living room from the hall.

I felt my cheeks grow hot. "Thanks, Nash."

"Everything okay with Rory?"

I nodded. "She should be out in a minute."

Just then, I heard a creak of the wood floors, and turned.

I felt my breath hitch. Her hair had slipped out of the pins in all the right ways while she'd changed. The dress was a perfect baby blue, and hugged her curves just like I'd hoped it would. The lace was as delicate as she was. God, she was the epitome of a princess, and I most definitely did not look good enough to call her my date.

"You look beautiful," I breathed.

Her cheeks flushed, and she grinned.

"Alright, well." Nash looked awkwardly between the two of us. "I'll meet you there, then."

"What?" I asked. "I thought you said car was here."

"I thought you might like your own."

I nodded, and he led the way outside to where Gordon was waiting next to a limo. I let out a gasp before rushing into his arms. I didn't care if Nash saw me do it. I had really missed this man.

"Alright, alright, don't go messing up your hair." Gordon laughed. "You look beautiful, Even."

"Thanks, G." I grinned, turning to where Rory was standing. "Gordon, this is Rory. Rory, this is Gordon, the best driver/Mario Kart racer to ever live."

"Mario…?" Rory began.

"Never mind."

"Take care of them, Gordon." Nash smiled, putting a hand on Gordon's shoulder before getting into the other limo out front.

"Always do, sir." Gordon smiled, outstretching his arm for us to climb in.

I'd tried to warn Rory about what would happen when she and I showed up, arm in arm. I'd tried to explain paparazzi to her. The flashing of the cameras, how you're supposed to pose and answer questions. But there isn't really any preparing you for how chaotic and invasive it is without seeing it first-hand.

Which is why all the flashing lights terrified her as Henry pulled up.

"Hey, it's okay," I said, taking her hand. "Remember, we do this together?"

Rory nodded, squeezing my hand twice.

Henry opened the door, and I stepped out. When I reached back for Rory, a wave of voices called my name. I was used to that. I'd dealt with that. Rory had not. She smiled anyway, and squeezed my hand twice again as we made our way to where a photo backdrop had been set up.

It was blindingly bright, each flash making it ten times worse. Every time I looked at Rory to make sure she was okay, she just squeezed my hand twice again, letting me know she was okay. Turns out, she was better at this than I was.

"Even!" I heard several shouts. "Even, is this your girlfriend? Are you confirming that you are part of the community? Do you have any response to the allegations that you were arrested before coming to France? Do you have any response to the allegations you were arrested *in* France? Are you attending boarding school in the fall?"

Both of us smiled. It wasn't normal for me to answer questions, even at the events. Sometimes I didn't even pose for the photos. Actually, I normally only posed for photos if Nash made me, but if the photo was of me and Rory, I'd pose for a thousand.

I was almost afraid the questions and photos would never stop when Nash's limo arrived. Marcus opened the door for him. There was a dramatic flare as he buttoned his suit jacket, then reached back into the car. For a moment, it was like the entire crowd held their breath until Autumn stepped out.

Oh, holy damn.

Autumn had always been pretty. But that night, she looked every bit as much like a princess as Rory. Her dark red hair was up, and the emerald green dress she'd donned made her look at least six inches taller. Wait, that was probably the heels.

Suddenly the wave of questions came toward Nash. Were they a couple? How did he know she was the one? Was there a ring? Were they expecting?

Rory and I tried making our way past the last few cameras when Nash called me.

"Need one of us together." He shrugged.

I nodded. They always did.

I stood next to Nash and put on my happy face. I was fine. This was fine. We were almost done. It was almost over.

"Even! Has your time in France prepared you for taking over the company?"

I felt my face fall. I looked up at Nash who had gone pale.

"What changes will you make as CEO?"

I was going to be sick.

"When were you going to tell me that the entire company would be mine at eighteen?" I shrieked in the hallway. "Nash, I'm not ready for this!"

"I'm sorry, Even." He sighed. "Listen, I was trying to get things sorted out for you. And I was trying to keep you out of the papers. That's why... that's why I brought you to France. I..."

"That's what you meant about him protecting me." I looked at Autumn.

She nodded slowly.

"It's not as scary as you're making it." Nash sighed. "It's going to be as simple as hiring a CEO."

"Oh, so *I* get to hire a CEO? I thought *you* were the CEO!"

"Your dad talked down his part in the company a lot, Ev. It was to protect you. He wanted you to have a normal life."

"What, so you're saying my dad was the company head, not you?" I couldn't believe this. My dad was home way too much for that to be true.

Nash sighed. "Yeah, he was, but the company was smaller then, and… he was a lot better at it than I am. I've been doing my best here, but the truth is that I was much better in IT than management. I'm a computers guy, not a CEO."

"And you think I'm going to be top-notch at management?"

"That's why I brought you in for the internship. I wanted to see what you could do with the work given to you—if you could connect with the mission of the company like your dad did. I thought maybe…"

"Maybe what? That I'd somehow move on faster because I was walking in my dad's shoes or something? Nash, I'm a musician. I draw and paint. I don't even know how to manage my mental health. I don't know the first thing about IT, much less running a company for it."

I felt my breath quicken. Oh, God. Not here.

"Hey," Rory said from behind me, her arm slid around my waist in that familiar way. "Let's go dance, hmm?"

Rory put her hand in mine, and I squeezed twice, nodding.

"Maybe all of us could use a dance," Autumn said, suddenly pulling Nash's attention away from me and Rory.

I wasn't ready to have this conversation. I wasn't ready to talk about the company. I just wanted to dance with my not-girlfriend and have one night out at the ball. Call me Cindereven, I didn't care.

When we finally made it into the ballroom, it was like a dream. The normal large meeting area had been completely transformed per our vision. Soft pink chiffon draped the ceiling, where vintage chandeliers hung across the room, and the dance floor had been brought in, a demask gold and white.

Rory gasped. "It's beautiful."

"Yeah, it is," I whispered, but I was looking at her when I said it.

She blushed as we made our way toward the dance floor. There was still dinner, speeches, and the auction, but for now, I just wanted to dance with Rory.

We caught some eyes as we started dancing that weird two or three step dance she'd shown me, but this was much slower. Compared to the other couples already there, we were dancing much more formally than their casual sway. People didn't dance like they had once upon a time.

It didn't stop us though. We kept dancing like that until the band stopped, which meant it was time to take our seats. The business part of the evening was about to begin.

I led Rory to the table, a part of the seating chart I'd set up myself. Rory was seated next to me, I was next to Nash, and Autumn next to him. I should have put Autumn between us. I hadn't thought about it. But, after the talk in the hall, I didn't think I was ready to sit next to him for the next hour. Nash stiffened as we took our seats. He apparently wasn't ready to talk, either.

Dinner was served as a woman I'd never met stepped up to the stage and began giving a layout for the night's events. She called Nash up to the stage to give a few words about, whatever Nash talked about. He was the CEO, after all. Correction; *acting* CEO.

He adjusted the buttons on his tuxedo as he stood and gracefully made his way to the stage. Nash was built for this sort of thing. He was suave. He was sophisticated. He had the swagger of a business man. How would I, a reckless teenager, ever amount to… that?

Nash was the right person to run this company. Just look at him. He was giving an amazing speech. He was talking about the company and our goals. He was calling me up to the stage.

He was calling me up to the stage?

There were eyes on me. Literally hundreds of eyes on me. I felt the blood drain from my face. I locked eyes with Nash, who was still looking at me expectantly.

"Even, will you come join me, please?" he repeated.

I let out a shaky breath, instinctively shaking my head. But I rose from my seat, nearly toppling it over with the poof of my dress. I couldn't just not go, that would cause a scene. I barely remember the walk to the stage, putting one foot in front of the other, avoiding the gazing eyes of those around us, trying not to pass out.

The light cast on the stage as I made my way to Nash was absolutely blinding. In an odd way, that was a relief, because I couldn't see the large crowd. The hard part was that it also meant I couldn't see Rory. I had a feeling seeing her would have helped me not want to puke.

"Many of you know of my charming niece." Nash smiled, placing an arm around my shoulders.

I offered a meek wave and swallowed hard. I wanted to stomp on Nash's toes and run as far away from here as possible. That would show him just how charming I could be. But I stayed put as he continued.

"Some of you are lucky enough to remember her father." Nash sighed, giving my shoulder a soft squeeze. "And others have only the chance to remember his memory. Even, who knew him probably the best of anyone, has taken this summer out of her busy schedule in Seattle to study as an intern with McCoy Enterprises."

I struggled to grin at the statement, which I'm sure was more of a grimace than anything else. It wasn't like I'd had a choice in the matter. Nash had forced the internship. Why was I up here?

"And she's spent most of her summer helping plan tonight's festivities, so the honor of host for this evening belongs to her and our esteemed new Public Relations head, Elaine Autry, here at the Lyon branch."

There was a bit of applause before the crowd quieted again. Nash clearly wasn't finished, as he hadn't taken his arm off my shoulder or made any motion to move. Shit, I wish he would. This was awkward for me.

"There has been talk with her upcoming age," Nash began, and I felt my heart begin to pound. What part of our literal screaming match in the hall made him think this was okay? "And with recent topics in the media, that our company might have a rocky future. Rest assured; McCoy Enterprises is in good hands."

Another spout of applause. Nash turned to me.

"Even, would you like to say anything?"

I felt my eyes go wide. His arm finally slipped off my shoulders as he stepped away from the microphone, gently pushing me toward it. I swallowed hard.

"But I—" I breathed, turning back toward the microphone.

I was grateful it wasn't making one of those awful ringing noises as I stood in front of it, looking out at the crowd. All I could really see was light shining back at me. I guess that was best.

"I'm not much for speeches," I nearly choked out, and there was a tiny gust of laughter. "Um… and I… I didn't prepare anything. So, um. Thank you… all for coming, and… um. I hope you enjoy the party, but don't forget the cause— the real reason we are here."

I nodded numbly, backing away from the light, and struggling to maintain a steady pace without falling or running back to my seat. Nash had already retaken his seat when I descended the stairs from the stage. Dinner was on our plates now, but I wanted to hurl.

Nash was smiling at me along-side Autumn when I made my way back. No one had taken the stage to say anything else. The auction wouldn't begin for a few more minutes. There were so many eyes on me, and the thought of retaking my seat made me shake.

So, I kept walking. I could feel my breath growing heavier. My hands were shaking. I could not stand a single moment longer in this crowd. My eyes were swelling. Fuck Nash. Fuck the company. And fuck this stupid party.

"Even?" I heard Nash call behind me.

Autumn's voice came after, but I couldn't hear what she said. I didn't care to. I needed out of here.

I'd only just reached the bathroom when I felt a hand wrap around mine. I didn't even have to see her to know it was Rory.

"Are you okay?" she asked, pulling me toward her gently.

I shook my head. I couldn't form the words to say why. Why Nash bringing me on stage upset me so much. Why him bringing up my dad was one of the worst things he could have ever done. Why him leaving me on stage felt a lot like a forecast for our future when I turned 18 and he handed the company to me.

Nash made me feel like everything this summer hadn't changed a thing between us. He was still using me for good press. He was still using my dad for good press. He just wanted everyone to think everything was a-okay. And the truth was that our family was broken. Our family was missing key members. I was a total disaster, and he was an absentee parent.

But saying all that out loud?

Rory didn't ask me to. She just pulled me into a hug and let me fall into the comfort that came with her arms around me. It was wordless. She didn't ask questions. She didn't pull away. She just held me.

It was me who pulled away, leaning down and kissing her. I pushed her against the marble wall of the women's bathroom, pinning her between my kiss and the cold stone. I needed her. I wanted her. Her hands were on my waist, but she only kissed me back for a moment before she pulled away.

"Even." *Please don't say my name like that.* "We should get back."

I let out a shaky breath, resting my forehead against hers and nodded.

When we returned to the hall, the auction had already begun. There was a large art piece on the stage, and people were raising their bid cards. Rory took my seat next to Nash, leaving a rather large gap between me and him. I didn't say anything, but I was trying hard not to smile.

Nash didn't say anything, but out of the corner of my eye, I saw him stiffen. Good. He knew I was upset with him, but he wasn't about to cause a scene here anymore than I was. We could both sulk in silence for the rest of the night.

As the auction pressed on, I pushed around the food on my plate until one of the servers came to get them, and I gladly handed it off. Rory was the only one to notice how little I'd eaten or how upset I still was. Meanwhile, it felt as if the rest of the table had moved on from the beginning of our evening. Nash was even bidding for things.

I couldn't be mad at him for that. All of this was for charity. The items had been donated, and even if all Nash seemed to be doing was driving up prices of things, him bidding just meant more money for the cause.

There was a meter running on the screen behind the stage as we made our way to the goal for the evening of a million dollars. I'd originally thought that goal was highly ambitious. No way could these people raise that much in one night. But just finishing the auction was over half, and that didn't even include the cost of each seat at the gala, which I'd also thought was outrageous. Why would people pay $1,500 for something like this?

According to Elaine, the summer gala in Lyon had cheaper seats than the ones at our other branches. I didn't want to know how much they were. Especially not since I'd attended them as a child growing up, which meant my parents had paid for their little kid to complain about the food and fall asleep halfway through the auction.

I was happy to see so many employees in attendance, though. Knowing employees didn't have to pay for their seats was reassuring. The company basically donated the money for anyone who wanted to go. I was pretty sure a lot of it came out of Nash's own pocket, but I was also sure he'd never admit to that.

When the auction came to a close, there was a series of thank-you speeches, and some talk of our upcoming year. Nash returned to the stage, and I ducked off to the bathroom. No way was I letting him call me up on stage again.

When I returned, Nash had retaken his seat, and the musicians who'd been performing during the beginning of the evening had taken over. The servers returned with a variety of desserts, and general conversation amongst the tables had resumed.

I let out a sigh as I took my seat next to Rory. The woman across from us, some higher up in Lyon, was talking to Nash. They were speaking in French, which surprisingly to me, wasn't as hard to understand as I'd expected.

She was asking about Rory, or rather, asking about Rory and me. Rory and I looked at one another through the corners of our eyes, and she reached over for my hand under the table. I took it. I was prepared for Nash to brush it off like usual. Rory was staying with us for the summer while things with her potential foster family were sorted out.

Instead, Nash told the woman Rory had been working with the company this summer along side me. Maybe to keep from embarrassing her? A lot of the people at the gala, and in the company, came from prestigious upbringings. Not that I couldn't say Rory had, too. He said she'd shown a lot of interest in public relations, and had even played a role in organizing the gala. We'd made fast friends.

Friends. *Friends.* Like we hadn't talked about Rory, and my feelings for her, at least a little. Like he hadn't seen the way she'd held my waist earlier, or the way we'd danced. Same old Nash.

When dessert was finished, dancing began again. Like I'd hoped, people were excited about my idea of casino-style games. Sure, people loved to dance, but not everyone did. Some people liked to gamble. Plus, that meant more money for the meter, which was all but full after some generous donations.

Personally, I couldn't wait to dance with Rory again, which surprised me. I think part of me also couldn't wait to get away from Nash again. I had a feeling the moment he caught me alone, we'd be having a talk. I was saved by some of the other party goers.

"Would you like to dance?" I asked Rory as Nash was pulled away from the table.

She nodded, and I took her hand. We joined the other couples on the floor. We twirled in circles until our legs grew tired, and our dresses seemed to have melded together until they'd become one.

Something about spinning her around the dance floor felt like that last dance between Disney Aurora and Prince Philip, but it was us. Two imperfect people enjoying a single night of bliss, even if we both knew that the credits weren't about to roll, and this wasn't the end. Life was more complicated than that, but that didn't mean tonight couldn't be a short and sweet happily ever after, did it?

She pressed her forehead to mine and just swayed with me for a while, letting me soak in all the comfort that being so close to her brought. The couples were dwindling. Donations had already been made, speeches done, and a lot of the more business aspects of the night were already over.

"Do you want to get out of here?" I whispered, pulling her attention back to me.

She nodded, and we slipped back out the way we'd come.

We made it to where the cars would pick us up, I spoke briefly to the valet, then we were just standing there, waiting, her hand in mine. She reached up and brushed a strand of hair from my face, and it was all I could do not to kiss her. We were alone, after all. So, I did.

But the moment her lips met mine, there was a flash from behind.

"I knew it!" the man said, as he darted backward toward the party.

"That doesn't sound good," Rory breathed, looking back at me.

I shrugged. "That's tomorrow's problem. Tonight is just for you and me."

Rory smiled slightly as the limo pulled up and we climbed in. Her lips were on mine again the moment we sat back in the car. Then they were trailing down my jawline, to my neck, my exposed collarbone. My heart was racing like each kiss sent a jolt to my system.

There was too much dress in the back of a limo for this. Too much dress, period. But somehow, her hands were still all over my body. It was the most lovingly wanted I'd ever felt. I was glad the barrier between us and the front was closed. I couldn't imagine having Gordon see *that* through the rearview. It would have been mortifying.

We didn't wait for Gordon to open the door before we climbed out. I called a thank you over my shoulder, and somehow managed to keep Rory's lips off mine long enough to get out of sight.

Once we were around the corner, Rory barely let me breathe long enough to unlock the door.

She tried starting to unzip my dress before we'd even made it to my room. That was the last thing I needed Nash to find. Him seeing us dance at the gala was one thing, and admitting I had feelings for her was another, but knowing we were intimate was something else entirely. I made her wait until we were in my room, with the door closed and locked before I let her remove anything from me or from herself.

Once that door was closed, the dress was gone. Hers, on the other hand, laced up the back, took a minute to remove, and I took pleasure in being meticulous about it. Mostly because I knew it was driving her crazy. Once she caught on, she wriggled out of it without my help and gave me a shove to the bed.

She climbed on top of me, looking down at my now bare chest, and whispered, "Are you sure?"

"Are you?"

"About you?" She leaned down, face inches from mine, the loose hair from her updo cascading around my cheeks. "Or about this?"

"Both."

"Yes."

"Then yes."

Her lips met mine again, and the next few moments were a blur of emotion with raging hormones. While her lips made their way to my jaw and neck again, her hands were slowly trailing their way down my midsection. My breath was heavy as she paused, her fingers just under the hem of my underwear.

Her eyes met mine for a brief second, just long enough that I had the chance to say no, ask her to slow down. I'd stopped her countless times at this point. I didn't this time, and she wasted no time after that.

I felt a moan escape my lips, and then my entire body was spasming, legs shaking, heart racing, all at the feel of her touch. She knew all the right places, all the right things, to push me over the edge, but she didn't. Once I was on the brink of bursting, she held me there.

"Even," she whispered, "Are you mine?"

"Yes," I gasped.

"Say it."

"I'm yours—"

The words were barely out of my lips before she was at it again.

The thing I never expected about sex was how much power you could give to someone else in one moment. In one single moment, you gave them power over your entire body. To love it, cherish it, and please it. Or, if you'd chosen the wrong person, break you entirely.

Rory kissed me again, and I rolled over with her onto my side. I was numb, dizzy, and blissful. It felt like the world was spinning.

"How do you feel?" she asked, brushing away the hairs from my face that had fallen out of my French twist.

I let out a breath. "I wish there were words."

She grinned.

I kissed her again, letting my hands slowly trail along her hips. She slowly pulled away, her hands reaching for mine.

"You don't have to," she whispered.

She almost looked afraid. Maybe she was as nervous as I was. I had no idea what I was doing, but that didn't tell me why she would be. Clearly, she knew more than I did.

"You don't want me to," I murmured, feeling my throat instantly go dry.

Blissful feeling gone. I was present again. She was still pulling away; still holding back. A part of her was still afraid of me. I felt like this might have been a mistake. If she couldn't trust me, open up to me, like I had for her, then why should I?

Before I could stop myself, my body shifted away.

"Even." Her hands slipped around my hips, pulling me closer to her. "I am just scared."

"Of me?"

"No, of this. Of what I feel for you because I… I have felt it before… and… and it hurt me. I could not bear to lose you too."

"Tell me about her." I swallowed hard. "Tell me about Catherine. Tell me what happened to you."

She looked at me for a moment, a familiar distant pain in her eye. It was a moment too long, and I knew I'd pushed too hard and asked the wrong question, but it was me who got up, pulled away, tried to end this conversation like she had so many times before. This time, it was I who was hurting and scared.

"Even." She sighed as I grabbed a t-shirt off the floor. "Wait…"

"For what, Rory?" I choked, grabbing a cigarette instinctively and shoving it between my lips. "You obviously can't trust me, even after I've told you the most painful parts of my past."

"Stop this. These smelly sticks are bad for you." She groaned. She got up and yanked the cigarette from my mouth, tossing it on the floor.

I bit my lip as she reached for my hands. "I am sorry." She sighed. "It was so long ago for you and so short for me. It still is hurting me."

"Maybe I can help, maybe I can—"

"No, it is my sorrow."

I scoffed, pulling my hands from hers. I grabbed the pack of cigarettes and had my hand on the handle of the door when she spoke.

"She was my maid."

I stopped, feeling my breath catch in my throat as I slowly let go of the door handle.

"She was kind and beautiful. And I loved her."

I turned to look at her. Her arms were crossed over her chest, and there were already tears in her eyes.

"It was me who moved first," she whispered. "I started it. And I knew what would happen if we were caught. I was promised to someone else the moment I was born. And to be with someone else, to be touched by anyone else... was forbidden. Things were different then. You and me, we could never have been. The church would never have allowed it."

She closed her eyes. "We were caught by my father himself."

I sucked in a shallow breath.

"The entire household knew within the hour. The people, they talk. There was no hope to keep the secret." She swallowed. "She was to be killed for defiling his daughter. And

I to be married off to the highest bidder who would have me. My betrothed did not want me when he learned I was no longer pure for him. And that is when my godmother stepped in."

I wanted to reach out and hold her, but something told me to stay put. A part of me was afraid that moving any closer would make her clam up again.

"We were both to sleep." She choked, two tears racing down each cheek. "And be together when we woke. Imagine my surprise when I wake to a kiss not from her, but from you."

"I'm sorry," I whispered.

"I will never know what happened to her." Her lip was quivering.

I crossed the room in a rush, dropping the cigarettes and pulling her into my arms instead. She sobbed into my shoulder, wrapping both arms around my waist. When she pulled away, she was still crying, but that didn't stop her from kissing me. It was greedy.

"Rory…" I said, pulling away. "It's okay."

"I love you."

"What?"

"I did not think I could." She sniffled, looking into my eyes. "But I love *you*, Even."

I kissed her. This time it was I who was hungry as I pulled her closer to me. I didn't really know why I was doing it. I just knew that hearing her say those words to me made me feel like I could do anything. Something about knowing you're loved makes you feel whole.

"Touch me," she whispered breathlessly against my lips. "Please."

I reached down and grabbed each of her thighs in my arms and carried her toward the bed like I'd seen in movies. She loved it. I was impressed with myself. Score one for me. The problem was that I still didn't know what I was doing, but Rory didn't seem to mind.

"It is okay," she whispered, pulling me closer by my shirt. "Do whatever you want."

◦◦◦

"How did she do it?" I whispered as I ran my fingers through Rory's hair.

The house was dark and silent now. Nash and Autumn hadn't come home, and I hoped that meant he was with her at the hotel. Having him come in now would be the cherry on the rocky part of our evening.

"Your godmother, I mean. Was she a witch like in the movie?"

"No." She sighed, her finger tips trailing up and down my thigh, leaving goosebumps in their wake. "She was of the Fae."

"The Fae?" I grinned. "They were real?"

"Mhmm. A lot of the old tales were true. Magic is still here, if only you look to find it."

"So, what did she do?"

"She told me I would be frozen until my love came to find me." She took a deep breath, and I was afraid I might have asked the wrong question again. "And I never thought that would mean a lifetime of sleeping."

"Or a few lifetimes."

She nodded.

219

"What about your family?" I asked. "Did you think you would miss them?"

She shook her head. "I would miss my godmother, but I barely knew my mother and father. I was choosing love."

"Do you wish it had been her?" I asked, feeling the very state of my heart hanging on the content of her response. "Instead of me."

"Not anymore." She looked up and kissed me softly before pulling away.

She drifted off to sleep not long after that, and like before I laid awake listening to the sound of her breathe. Every beautiful part of that night was torn to pieces by the word she mumbled in her sleep.

Catherine.

Chapter 30

The next morning's headline was staring me in the face along with a rather impressive photo of Rory's lips on mine. It wasn't the first time I'd been on the cover, and it probably wouldn't be the last, but this one felt far too personal for my liking.

Out McCoy Enterprises' Heiress Leaves Party Early With Mystery Date: True Love or Summer Fling?

"Ev, do you have a minute?" Nash asked from the kitchen doorway.

I nodded, taking a sip of my coffee, and putting down the paper that had come that morning. I was tired of looking at it, anyway. It was mocking me, reminding me that I wasn't anyone's true love. I was what they settled for.

Nash sighed. "I need to know where your head is at."

"Look, Nash, I've got a few more months to think about the company, right?"

"No, not about that. About Rory."

I bit my lip. I was not ready to talk about Rory to Nash. I wasn't even ready to talk about her to her.

"You knew this was temporary," he continued. "You're here on a summer work visa. And I've spent these last three weeks trying to get Rory set up here, so she can find a foster family, get enrolled in school, and have a future."

I nodded, feeling myself go numb.

"But I gather there are some real feelings between the two of you now."

I looked down. "I didn't choose to like girls."

"Even," he groaned. "It's not about you being gay. I figured that out a while ago. It's about Rory specifically."

"What about her?"

"She's French, Even. And you spent the entire summer trying to ensure you could finish school in Seattle. We leave in three days. Is that still what you want? Or—"

"Of course, it is." I sighed.

"Does she want to come to Seattle?" he asked, hesitantly. "Because I'm sure I could find a way to make that work."

I shook my head. I didn't know. I didn't want to know.

"I mean I knew this was temporary." Not letting my voice crack took all my willpower. "I shouldn't have let things go so far, anyway."

No one leaves their home for their second choice. There was no happy ending here. I should have known that. Hell, I did know that, and I let myself fall for her anyway.

"I'm not going to tell you what to do here. I don't feel like it's my place. But you and Rory might sit down and talk about it. We've found her a foster family, and we have to give them an answer by the end of the week."

He turned to leave, and we both looked up to find Rory standing in the doorway eyes darting between us both. There were tears in her eyes. She stormed out of the room.

She wouldn't open the door for me, not that I was surprised. It was Nash who finally got her to talk to him, and hear what he had to say. She told him one thing that really shattered my heart. France is her home.

It hurt, not because I didn't know it was true, but because in the few weeks since she'd begun calming the storms of my dreams, she'd become my home. Or, at least, the closest feeling of home I'd felt since my parents had died. Knowing that I wasn't that for her was worse than knowing I would never measure up to who she'd really wanted to wake her.

I felt a turning in my gut as I closed and locked my door. Tearless sobs came first, then the tears came second. My feet gave out as I slipped onto the floor. If either of them heard me, they didn't come to the door to say anything. Perhaps that hurt the most.

Chapter 31

I wasn't prepared for how empty I would feel lying in my bed alone again after weeks of drifting off to the rhythm of Rory's heartbeat. I wasn't prepared for the fear that came with the nightmares that she couldn't keep at bay if she wasn't even here. I wasn't prepared for how alone I felt waking up from them now that I knew I might never have that feeling of safety again. And I wasn't prepared for how much I would ache to tell her about it.

The foster family picked up Rory the next morning. She wouldn't say goodbye to me, and I couldn't blame her. A part of me didn't want to either. Leaving things as they were, unspoken, was simpler and less painful.

The ride to work was lonely; even Henry seemed sad. The things we passed didn't look the same without seeing them with her. France wasn't France without Rory. I'd never been more ready to go back to Seattle.

"Where is Rory?" Madam Caron asked as I stepped in.

It was my last day. I couldn't imagine she had a lot of work left for me, especially not with the gala behind us. I was pretty sure this was just a formality.

"She's gone." I swallowed hard. "Her foster family picked her up today."

"Mmm?"

The frown on her face gave me pause. I knew her and Rory had grown close in the last few weeks, but I didn't think it was that serious.

"She is not staying with you?" she asked.

I shook my head. "I'm going back to Seattle, and France is her home. We both knew this was just temporary."

"My office, *mon cherie.*"

My heart raced as I followed her into the glass box, she called an office. Sound proof, sure, but with all the bustle outside of it, I couldn't imagine how she got anything done. Though, I rarely saw her in there, anyway.

"Tell me." She sighed as she shut the door. "Did you wake her?"

I sucked in a shallow breath. "I'm sorry, what?"

"Aurora. Did you wake her?"

I swallowed and nodded. There was no sense in lying. She clearly knew, but I wasn't exactly sure how.

"What did you think that would mean?"

"I don't—"

"She waited all this time… for *you.*" Madam Caron looked tired as she leaned against her desk and peered down at me. "I doubted at first that you could be the one, but I saw something in you the day you brought in those coffees. A… drive to prove yourself. And I saw as you began learning French that you are not someone who gives up easily."

"I'm not." I swallowed hard. "But she doesn't want me. I'm not who she wanted to wake her up, and whatever she thinks she feels, deep down I'll always be second to Catherine."

"What do you know of Catherine?"

It wasn't condescending. It was just a simple question. I sighed and looked down.

"Not a lot." I shrugged.

"Catherine left her, Even," she scoffed, causing me to look back up. "Catherine was to join her in the tower, and they would wake when it was safe. Instead, she ran."

"Why?"

"That is the question. Perhaps it was love for Aurora, but something less for Catherine." Madam Caron shrugged, and there was a glint in her eye. I never thought I would see this fierce, intimidating woman show even the slightest weakness.

"You're her godmother," I breathed.

She nodded.

I had so many questions. Starting with how she was still alive after all these years. Did the Fae live that long? Why she was working for McCoy Enterprises? But I felt like so many of them were the wrong ones to ask.

"Why me?" I asked finally. "Are we bound by destiny or something?"

"*Non.* The spell was simple. She would sleep until a heart worthy of her found her. So, here you are, doubting yourself, but magic does not lie. And it wasn't the spell that made her love you. It was you."

"I'm not so sure she loves me." I bit my lip, looking down.

"This?" She picked up the newspaper I'd been eyeing the morning before. "Is not the face of someone in like. Was I wrong about you? Have you given up so easily?"

Chapter 32

Every piece of clothing I folded and tucked into my suitcase that afternoon sent a wave of guilt washing over me, as the conversation I'd had with Madam Caron turned over and over in my mind. There was no way to contact Rory or her foster family, not until Nash got home, and he wasn't answering his phone.

When I'd gone across the floor earlier, the receptionist said he was at a worksite. She wasn't sure when he'd return, but would leave a message for him. Henry didn't know where the foster home was, either. That meant packing was pretty much all I could do.

No matter what happened, I wasn't staying here in this house after tomorrow. No matter what happened. Like I could somehow change Rory's mind. Like I could somehow change my own. Even Madam Caron hadn't completely convinced me. You couldn't deny what someone said in their sleep.

Eventually, I was just crying as I packed, and I found myself wandering the house. I went to the spare room first. Something about knowing Rory had been here, slept here, sat in this very window sill made me feel slightly better. Or worse, I couldn't be sure. I was still crying, so it obviously wasn't helping.

It smelled like her. I couldn't put my finger on what it was; it was just Rory. That gave me the feeling of home that made my heart ache. I'd only just turned to leave when a bound leather book caught my eye.

Her journal.

There were plenty of fancy things in the tower when I'd found her, and this book was the only thing she'd chosen to keep. Why would she leave it behind?

It was open when I walked over to it, open to one of the last pages, like she'd filled the entire thing in the last twelve weeks. Maybe she had. It wasn't like I'd seen her writing in it, but she often told me she couldn't sleep. Maybe this is what she did with her time. This page, though, was addressed to me.

My Even. I swallowed hard at reading that. I was hers. That's what I'd said.

I know that you do not believe in fairytales, but I want you to know that you still gave my story the happily ever after it deserved. And because I like the irony, I am going to tell you a story; my story.

Once upon a time, there lived a beautiful princess born to a stubborn and cruel king and queen. The king brought home his troubles from war, and the queen lived a life of pure vanity. They were disliked among the whole kingdom.

They never took the time to know their child, but rather, tried to mold her into the person they wanted her to be. The queen insisted on beauty, and the king insisted on silence and obedience. And nothing the princess did was good enough for either of them.

They saw her as only a pawn. A means to a better end for their kingdom. With a marriage to a prince in a distant land, the kingdom would thrive. And while the princess wanted to do what was right for her people, the prince was terrible, and she knew she would never love him.

The only solace she found was in the care of her godmother, who told her stories of the Fae and their magic. She promised her that one day, the princess would find true love. And she promised that the prince was not who she would marry.

So, she loved, hard and passionately, turning to anyone who gave her any mind, until she found someone who loved her back. But when the king learned of her disobedience, his rage took over. He beat her until her body was black and blue. He promised to sell the princess like livestock and kill her love.

It seemed that no true love could withstand the evil in her home. That was, until her godmother gave her a choice. Magic comes at a price, and this spell would mean there was a chance she would find true love, but also a chance she would only find heartbreak. All she had to do was sleep.

And so she slept, with dreams of a better future running through her mind until she was woken by a beautiful stranger. A stranger who looked so much like her lost love it ached the very pit of her heart, and somehow gave her hope. Hope that this really was her true love.

Because that was the promise her godmother had given.

I do not know if you are my true love, or if true love does exist, but I do know that you are the love of my life. And for that, a part of me will always be yours.

Love always,

Aurora,

And Even, never stop playing the piano.

At the back of the book, next to the page I'd just finished reading were two drawings. One with my name on it, and one with Catherine's. The resemblance was uncanny. There were only minor differences in the height of our cheek bones and the width of our noses. I didn't even know Rory could draw.

As I leafed back through the book, I saw that she had been writing all summer. She'd been writing about me. This book contained every moment we'd had together, her retellings of how she fell in love with me.

But further back, in that section of old French I'd struggled to read before, I could make out some things. Stories about her old life, her old home, her old love. Maybe it wasn't right to read it, but she'd left it here for me to find. I couldn't say for sure what she'd want.

She had loved Catherine in that first love, head over feet, "risk it all on a pipe" dream kind of way. But Catherine didn't love her back. It was obvious even in her own writing that Catherine was playing a part.

From what she wrote about hearing me tell Nash this was temporary, she thought I didn't love her either. I felt a turning in my gut.

∽⬡∾

Nash still wasn't answering, and I was getting annoyed. I'd called him ten times while pacing the living room. I needed to get ahold of Rory. I needed to tell her the truth about how I felt.

Eventually I stopped pacing and sat down on the piano bench, slowly hashing out one half of the Heart and Soul duet. It was sad and pathetic. Until somehow, I ended up going through my recital piece, crying through the last half, but I still remembered it. Every single note.

"I had no idea you could play like that."

I jumped and immediately started wiping my eyes. "I messed up twice."

"Could have fooled me." He smiled, a half-smile, but it made me feel a little better. "I saw you called, everything okay?"

"Yeah, I just needed to talk to you about—"

His phone rang. He let out an exasperated huff.

"I'm sorry, I have to take this."

Typical. Just when I really needed to say something, Nash absolutely *had* to take a phone call. This summer really hadn't changed much. It was already so late, it was unlikely I'd be able to talk to Rory, anyway.

When Nash stepped back into the room, his face was pale.

"What?" I asked.

"Rory's missing."

Chapter 33

There was a turning in my gut as I ran to my room and threw on a pair of shoes and grabbed my pepper spray. Nash was following me. He was saying something, but I wasn't really listening. My mind was too busy racing about all the places Rory could be. Where would mean the most to her? That's where I needed to start.

"Where are you going?" Nash asked, eyeing me. "Do you know where she could be?"

"The tower." I mumbled without thinking. *Shit.*

"The tower? What tower?"

"We don't have time to talk about it, Nash, I have to go."

"Well, I'm coming with you. Henry's left for the night anyway."

I started to groan, but choked it down. I didn't want him thinking I was angry. Nash coming with me meant explaining where we were going, why, and what it all meant. It wasn't like I could tell him the truth, but it didn't appear that he was giving me much choice.

The two of us raced to the car and climbed in, with me telling Gordon where to go.

"This will take us toward the reserve." Nash frowned. "She couldn't have possibly—"

"She could, and I'm sure she did," I replied. "Turn here. Could you step on it a little?"

"Ev, where are we going, what tower?"

"It's complicated."

"Uncomplicate it."

"I can't without—" I sighed.

"Without what?"

"Not without telling you who she is."

"Well, who is she?" He nearly snorted. "Who is Rory?"

"You wouldn't believe me if I told you. Take a left."

"Try me."

I swallowed hard and shook my head. "Believe me, Nash. It's not worth trying."

"Even, tell me the truth." He was serious now. His tone of voice had deepened well past any hint of lightheartedness. "If she's in some kind of trouble—"

"It's not like that."

"Then what is it like?"

I looked up at him. He had that same look my dad had given me all the times I'd lied to him as a kid, which wasn't many. The "you can trust me" face that made me want to spill all my secrets. I felt my eyes swell, because no way was he going to believe this.

"Even, you can trust me." That did it.

I was crying, like really crying. I wanted to trust him. I wanted to tell him the truth and for him to believe me, but I knew that wasn't possible. The truth was so absolutely unbelievable.

Runaway? Believable. Orphan? Also, totally believable. Daddy issues? No problem. But convincing Nash that Rory was Sleeping Beauty awoken from a spell 600 years later? No way in hell.

"Ev." He sighed, trying to pull me closer, but I had to keep my eyes on the road. "Whatever it is, we can sort it out."

"Turn right here," I said between sobs.

"My job is to protect you. Whatever it is, I'll believe you."

I was trying to slow my breathing as we rushed down the dirt road. It was so dark; I could barely see a thing. But the headlights flashed across a break in the trees.

"That's it!" I called. "Stop here."

I flung open the door and was halfway out of the car when Nash grabbed my wrist.

"You can't just rush off into the woods at night! Are you crazy?"

"Rory's out there," I breathed. "I'm sure of it. You said I can trust you. Can you trust me?"

"It's not you I don't trust, it's whatever could be in those woods." He still hadn't let go of my wrist.

"Give me fifteen minutes, and if I'm not back, you can send the calvary in after me." I forced a smile. "Please, Nash. Trust me."

"Tell me who she is first." He smirked. He was about to let me win. All I had to do was to let him in first.

"She's Aurora." I sucked in a shallow breath. "*That* Aurora."

He frowned, a puzzled look washing over his face, but his grip on my wrist loosened just enough for me to slip free and rush into the woods before he could stop me. He was still wearing his suit, and fancy shoes. I knew better than to think he would follow me on his own. I didn't even think he'd grabbed his phone.

The first trip across this footpath had been slow. Cigarette in hand, I was merely looking to blow off steam. I took my time meandering along.

I wasn't walking this time; I was running. It had been a while since I'd run like that, and I quickly realized I was out of shape.

I kept pushing anyway, pushing past the pain in my side, the ache in my feet, and the tension in my legs. Using the light from the crappy phone Nash had given me, I struggled not to stumble against the forest floor. Branches crossed the path, roots pushed up out of the ground. I was lucky I didn't fall as the pathway broke off, and the dirt trail looked more and more familiar.

The moonlight was bright enough now that I almost didn't need the flashlight.

When I reached the spot where I'd seen the orb, I was awestruck. The tower was gone. No vines leading up a stone wall. No crumbled stone lying about. It was completely gone. A clearing with a single tree in the center was in its place, like it had never been here in the first place. Like I'd never been locked inside. Like I hadn't woken Rory up at all.

A swell of panic consumed me, making it almost impossible to catch my breath after the run through the woods. She wasn't here. There was nothing here—nothing but trees as far as I could see. I had no idea where else she would have gone.

I clenched my jaw, reared back, and punched a nearby tree. Pain raced up my arm, and a cry escaped my lips before I could stop it. Stupid. Why was I so stupid?

I heard an audible gasp. "Even?"

Near the center of the clearing, beneath that single tree, Rory was struggling to stand.

I ran to her.

"Oh my God," I whispered as I threw my arms around her shaky shoulders. I tried not to wince as my hands clashed together. "Are you okay?"

She sniffled against my shoulder, but didn't pull away. "It's gone. It's all gone."

"It's okay," I breathed, pulling away and brushing the hair from her face with my good hand. "You don't need to go back."

"There's nothing for me here."

"Look at me. I'm right here. You have me. I'm yours, remember?"

"You're leaving," she cried. "You're leaving, and you don't love me."

"Yes, I do." I let out a painful laugh. "I do love you. And I'm not going anywhere."

"What? You said the Washington was your home."

"*You're* my home. And if that means a French boarding school, online tutors, or whatever Nash can come up with, I'm fine with that. My home is wherever you are."

"You'd stay for me?"

"Yeah, I would." I smiled. "I'm gonna take care of you."

Her hands wrapped around my neck as she pulled my face to hers and kissed me. When they talk about breath taking kisses taking control of your entire body and rocking your hardware, this was one of those. It took physical effort to pull away.

"Wait. Wait." I let out a shaky breath. "I have to text Nash or he will seriously call in a search and rescue."

I sent a quick text. **Found her. We are safe.**

"Are you ready to get out of here?" I asked, brushing hair from her face, if only for the ability to touch it.

She nodded slowly, and took my hand. My good hand.

"I know what happened to Catherine, by the way." I sighed as we made our way back toward the footpath. "You were right about Madam Caron. You did know her."

Next to me Rory smiled, leaning her head against my shoulder.

Chapter 34

I don't think I'd ever seen Nash as worried as he was the moment before we came into view. His jacket was removed, tie pulled out, top buttons undone, and sleeves rolled up. He was pacing, his phone firmly pressed between his cheek and shoulder. This might have annoyed me, him being on the phone, had it not been for what he said into it.

"Oh, thank God," he murmured the moment we came into view. "They're back. Yes, both of them. No, they look fine. I'll see you when we get back."

Nash pulled me into another hug. He was doing that a lot lately, which was weird, but I accepted it anyway.

"What were you thinking?" he asked Rory. "You could have gotten hurt."

Then he hugged her too. She tensed up at first, but relaxed into his arms like I had. Despite his typically gruff, business-like approach to life, he gave some good dad hugs. Maybe there was hope for Nash after all.

We loaded back into the car, and Rory's hand slipped into mine as the car started. I winced. She looked down at my bruised knuckles and met my eyes before letting out a sigh and shaking her head.

She didn't let go of my hand, though. Despite how much it hurt, I didn't mind.

Nash pulled his phone back out and started dialing. I tried not to be annoyed. It wasn't like it was surprising anymore. Only, it was.

"Hey Diana, it's Mr. McCoy. I have some good news." Nash said quickly. "Yes, we found her. She's alright... I was wondering if I might have a word with you regarding her custody situation."

Nash and I locked eyes.

"Yeah, I think I'd like to start the process. I'm sure we can do more good for her than the system."

My eyes swelled. I tried to blink them back. Shit, the last thing I wanted Nash to see was me blubbering like a baby again. But I couldn't help it.

"That would be great," he continued, looking ahead again. "No, I can send someone to fetch them, that's not a problem at all."

Nash didn't say anything else as we pulled in front of the house. Rory hadn't let go of my hand, which was still throbbing, but I didn't dare complain.

Autumn met us in the doorway, and she pulled each of us into a hug, giving Rory two. I knew something had changed about Nash that summer, but it wasn't until I saw the two of them talking next to the car that I realized what had changed.

It was Autumn. He was softer around her. His whole demeaner changed. He listened to her, and he really heard her. Now it was like he was listening to others better too.

There was food waiting on the table when Rory and I stepped inside. The whole table was set. I knew both Autumn and Nash wanted to talk and celebrate, but all I wanted was to hold her. I could say I wasn't going anywhere all I wanted, but I knew she wouldn't believe it unless I showed her.

"Oh," Rory breathed when she walked into the room. "I am not—"

"You're eating," Autumn insisted from the front door. "I'm not taking no for an answer."

Rory nodded, taking a seat quietly. A silence settled over the four of us as everyone sat down. I reached for her hand under the table, and she offered a weak smile.

"It's going to be okay," I insisted.

She gave my hand a squeeze before picking up her fork and pushing her food around. I don't think we got around to celebrating. Rory was tired, I was tired, Nash had more phone calls to make.

Rory fell asleep fast. Maybe the day had worn her out, or maybe it was simply a feeling of safety. I laid awake into the night, just listening to the sound of her breathing. I don't know what I was waiting on. Maybe reality to pinch me, let me know that I didn't win. I don't get to be this happy.

It never came.

The next morning, Nash was in the kitchen when I got up for coffee. Rory was sleeping in late. Autumn was in Nash's room, which I really didn't want to talk to him about. But it meant we had time to talk, just the two of us.

"How is she this morning?" he asked as he flipped the page on the newspaper.

Rory and I were no longer the cover. News had moved on to bigger and better things. No one cared about us now, and that was nice. A quiet happily ever after was much better to me.

"Still sleeping." I shrugged as I poured some coffee. "I don't suppose that's a bad thing."

"Not necessarily, gives us time to talk."

I stiffened instinctively. "What about?"

"Well," he sighed, taking a sip of his coffee and putting down the paper. "What do you want to do next? What's your game plan?"

"Oh."

I let it hang there. The truth was, I didn't know. What was my game plan?

"You still need to finish school." He turned in the seat so he could see me better.

Maybe I was a jerk for not sitting down.

"Yeah... about that." I let out a sigh. "I don't think... I don't think I want to go back to Rainer Beach."

"I agree." He tapped the side of his cup with his ring. "I think after the progress you've made, going back where your old friends were, that's just asking for trouble. I'd actually looked into a school here."

"You what?"

"It's fine if you're not interested, but between the comments I heard from Madam Caron, and what Autumn said about Rory, you just seemed… happy here. And I thought there was a chance you might not want to leave."

"I am happy here." I nodded. "I guess a part of me doesn't want to leave, but I do miss Seattle."

He nodded, "You don't have to decide today, Ev, but soon. And I think you should keep your options open. I suppose Rory has a say in things as well now."

"Yeah." I grinned. "I'll be happy as long as she is."

I had been happy here with Rory. I'd felt loved and wanted and at peace. But all of that had been Rory, too. *She* made me feel all those things. I guess I could have gone anywhere with her, and Nash might have thought the exact same thing.

Madam Caron stopped by later that morning, holding a file she passed on to Nash.

"What's this?" he asked.

"Some things of Rory's. I'm sure she'll be needing them." She smiled at him.

Before he could offer anything but a meek "thank you" his phone was ringing. He headed off into the hallway, talking loudly like usual.

Rory gave Madam Caron a tight hug. "I knew it was you."

Madam Caron grinned wide.

"I don't believe it." Nash laughed. "They found Rory in the system! Paul said they must have over-looked it the first time; something about a trainee using the wrong spelling."

Madam Caron gave us both a wink at that statement, then she pulled me aside.

"How are you feeling?" she asked. "About you and Rory and your future together."

"Better." I nodded, but I knew it wasn't genuine enough, because her face softened.

"Has she told you how much you look like—"

"Yes," I scoffed, but I was smiling nervously as I did it. I wasn't trying to be rude, but I didn't think I could handle hearing her name again. Not just yet.

"When I saw her growing old with someone she loved, I thought it was her." Madam Caron sighed, eyeing me with an all-knowing smile. "But now I see, it was you."

She didn't say anything else, but then again, she didn't have to. She'd said we'd grow old together. Me and Rory would grow old together. And with only those words, and my new found belief in magic, true love, and the possibility of the impossible, suddenly my fears about losing her to something stupid like a car crash melted away.

"You did it, little one," she said as she turned to Rory and offered her a warm hug.

I never thought I'd see something so motherly from a person who'd terrified me so much in the beginning.

"I did what?" Rory asked as she pulled away, looking up.

"You're free now." Madam Caron smiled. "You can just be, and be happy. I'm glad I was here to see it."

"Thank you, for everything. But why... why do I fear I'll never see you again?"

"Oh," She tutted. "I must return to the Fae. I've stayed away for so long, little one. I must return home, just as you must make one here, together."

"You were just waiting... for me." Rory sniffled, wiping tears from her face.

Madam Caron nodded. "I had to see that you were safe. I had to know it worked. I couldn't have planned it better myself."

She looked at me and gave me a wink.

"I must be off," she sighed, holding Rory's hands in her own. "Take care of her, yes?"

She wasn't looking at either of us when she said it, but rather between us, as if the question was directed at us both. We nodded, and she turned to leave.

As she pulled away, Rory was in tears, tucked under my arm, and clinging to my midsection, but she insisted it was okay.

"It's okay if you're not," I whispered into her hair. "It's okay... it's okay not to be okay."

"I am." She sniffled. "Just knowing she was here all that time, watching over me... that's what I needed. All I really wanted was the chance to say goodbye, and I have... to her, at least."

That would never happen for her and Catherine. Catherine, who we both now knew had chosen to run rather than be with her. Catherine, who Rory assured me was in her nightmares, not her dreams. Catherine who was her past, while I... I was her future.

Being her future was perhaps the best feeling of it all.

The file Madam Caron had given Nash contained Rory's real identification papers. Big shocker there. I wonder where she could have cooked those up. I was thinking more magic, but she'd never admit to that, not to me, and especially not to Nash.

Having them meant Rory wasn't on some waitlist. She wasn't an asylum seeker or an immigrant. They proved she was French, with a French ID, French birth certificate, and French passport.

Suddenly the world was wide open.

Chapter 35

We were surrounded by boxes and bare pink walls. Gone were the posters I'd once hung, the photos I'd taped up, and the flyers from bands I barely even remembered. I was packing away the last of what remained of my things at the penthouse. Pretty much everything else was already gone.

Autumn wasn't a fan of how large it was, and these days, what Autumn loved was the only thing Nash cared about. So, they purchased a five-bedroom house in the suburbs, and most of the ridiculous lavish furniture here was being donated.

"Are you ready, Even?" Rory called from the other room.

"Yeah, I'm finishing the last box." I stuffed my hoodie inside and forced it to shut so I could tape it.

"Want some help?"

"Sure."

"I'm still surprised to see you have a pink room." She grinned up at me.

"I didn't pick it." I stuck my tongue out at her and headed toward the door.

Rory chased after me, her arms wrapping around my waist just as I reached the door. I felt a laugh escape my lips as we came into view of Nash and Autumn. They were both on their phones. I rolled my eyes.

"Are you two not ready?" Nash chuckled slightly over his email. "You very well might miss your flight."

"Oh tra-la." I scoffed audibly. "The private plane might leave without us."

"It might, I'll send Daren a text now."

The smirk on his face told me he would do no such thing, but Autumn was amused nonetheless.

"Oh, let them reminisce." Autumn sighed. "I'm sure there are things Even will miss about this place."

"No, actually, if I could have convinced him to sell the place the moment I stepped foot into it, I would have. But Rory over here does love the view."

"The Seattle is so beautiful." Rory sighed next to me, her eyes out the large picture window.

I kissed her temple, turning back to Nash. "What about you, are you going to miss anything about this place?"

He let out a sigh and finally put his phone down, looking around at the now nearly empty apartment. He shook his head. "If I'm honest, and it pains me to be so, I wasn't around enough to miss it." We locked eyes. "More negative memories here than good ones."

I nodded. Same for me, but I wouldn't say that out loud. This house had meant mostly lonely nights, dinners alone, or screaming matches between the two of us. There was very little I remembered about the penthouse that was actually positive, and leaving it behind was like throwing out the trash.

"Alright," Autumn chimed. "The movers are set to be here by morning. All your boxes are marked?"

I nodded. "Big, bold, blue letters. Hard to miss."

"I can't believe you're going to college already!" Autumn chirped as she crossed the room to me with open arms.

I let her hug me. I was getting more used to those now.

It had only taken me six weeks with a private tutor to finish my senior year of high school, which impressed the hell out of Nash, because he didn't realize my grades had been low not because I wasn't smart, but because I didn't give a damn. Given the chance to jump on through, get my diploma, and move on with my life with Rory, I worked my ass off.

She was worth trying for.

Rory, on the other hand, had a bit longer in the schooling department. She was brilliant, a quick study, and basically loved the idea of devouring information, but she was still behind on so much that she'd missed. Some of which couldn't be taught in books. The good news was that we had time.

So, Rory would be working on high school while I attended college. And maybe, maybe I'd consider working with the company. For now, Nash seemed pretty confident he could handle things, at least until I had a degree under my belt. Whether that was business or music, he didn't quite seem to care.

That was our story. How one summer, in a hidden forest in France, I woke sleeping beauty.

Anyway, that was a much longer story than I meant it to be, but I know you're not crazy. Because if I can wake Sleeping Beauty after she'd slept 600 years, there's no way your Beast could surprise me.

About the Author

Elizabeth Jeannel was born and raised in Southwest Missouri. Her parents, who divorced when she was two, were both English majors, and avid readers, during her childhood.

While her mother read her fairy-tales, The Chronicles of Narnia, and an array of other child friendly books, her father put most of his focus on introducing comic books at a young age. Because of this, she was never without a book at arms reach.

Her love for reading quickly transformed into a love for writing. She wrote her first short story at age ten, and decided then she wanted to become an author.

Today, Elizabeth shares a home in Southwest Missouri with her wife and their fur children. She is the author of The Travelers series, The Art of Feeling, and Cursed (the novella). She currently has two novels in the works, and is participating in National Novel Writing Month on a yearly basis.

Also by Elizabeth Jeannel

You can find more information about
Elizabeth Jeannel and her upcoming books
and events at www.elizabethjeannel.com

Made in the USA
Middletown, DE
13 August 2020